Valerie pulled the e

Shhhhwwwwooooommmmm! Like a rocket, she shot straight up and out of the SuperCopter, the sweet, salty air rushing from her lungs. The wind rushed around her as the air pulled tears from her eyes. Her short, brown hair wrapped around her face. Suddenly she began to reverse direction toward the water below.

Fpppaaapppp! A small parachute popped out of the top of the chair. Valerie was jerked upward again, and a large metal ring from the base of the chair dropped off. Then she began to drift downward. Valerie opened her eyes. The ocean below rolled in ... ack against ... heart sk... into her own ... d of metal s...

Val... *ely he ejec...*

She... en the oce... At once, s... waves ... found t... ps popped ... left it on as ... fined. T... the moving...

Vale... ters hadn't s... save Al...

Look for these other books in the *Commander Kellie and the Superkids*$_{SM}$ Series!

#1 — *The Mysterious Presence*

#2 — *The Quest for the Second Half*

#3 — *Escape From Jungle Island*

#4 — *In Pursuit of the Enemy*

#5 — *Caged Rivalry*

#6 — *Mystery of the Missing Junk*

#7 — *Out of Breath*

Commander Kellie and the Superkids℠

#7

Out of Breath

Christopher P.N. Maselli

KENNETH
COPELAND
PUBLICATIONS

Out of Breath

ISBN 1-57562-660-8 30-0907

08 07 06 05 04 03 7 6 5 4 3 2

Kenneth Copeland Publications
Fort Worth, Texas 76192-0001

For more information about Kenneth Copeland Ministries, call 1-800-600-7395 or visit www.kcm.org.

cover art by John Shallenberger

Dedication

For Carol Fox, editorial genius, who has worked harder on these books than anyone—including me.

And for "Brother Larry" Warren and John Shallenberger, whose detailed cover art always takes my breath away.

Contents

Dear Superkid,

A Pacific Ocean sunset... The surprise of seeing a falling star... A warm hug when I'm feeling lonely... These things always take my breath away. Of course, I'm speaking figuratively—because actually having to hope and pray for your next breath is unnerving, to say the least. I know. And it's an experience I prefer to never repeat again.

I'm Valerie Rivera, and recently I was sent on a mission that left me gasping for breath more than once. Oh yes, it was an adventure—almost completely *under* the sea—which made it quite different from any I've ever had.

When I'm not adventuring, I live at Superkid Academy, which is my training ground for a life of adventure with God. I attend the Academy with my friends Paul, Missy, Rapper and Alex. Together, we make up the Blue Squad. Our leader is Commander Kellie. The six of us have been on many adventures—and I'm sure God has many more in store for us.

But going on an adventure that put me out of breath more than once made me face some hard realities in my life... Thank God, I had His protection and His Word to guide my way.

So are you prepared to dive into an underwater adventure where sharks are rampant and pirates make the rules? Get ready...because you're about to discover what it's like when you find yourself out of breath!

Valerie

Out of Breath

1

Ready to Dive?

A deep breath of crisp, salty, ocean air filled Valerie's lungs. As she slowly exhaled, she felt great. The taste of the air reminded her of her childhood home on Calypso Island. One thing she really missed about that little island was waking up with the freshness of the sea air in her lungs.

It would be awhile before she'd go back to Calypso—and, truth be known, Valerie had no plans to return permanently. Her Caucasian mother and Hispanic father were missionaries and they raised their daughter on the island—for which Valerie had no regrets. But her life had changed now. She still felt the family calling to missionary work, but hers would be at Superkid Academy—taking on the role as commander and raising up her own Blue Squad. At least that was Valerie's dream.

"There is nothing up here," Valerie's 11-year-old friend, Alex, said. His round, dark face was addressing her from a small, digital view-screen in the SuperCopter's dashboard.

Valerie punched a light-blue, rectangular button and

shook her head. She looked at the sweeping, green radar. It was almost completely blank; there was nothing out there. Valerie's SuperCopter was a small, fluorescent-green blip. Alex's SuperCopter was another dot—a few hundred meters behind Val's.

"I'm not really sure what we're looking for," Alex admitted.

Valerie shrugged her shoulders, feeling the crisscrossing seat belt straps tug at them. The dark blue, Superkid flight uniforms weren't the most comfortable uniforms from the academy. The lightweight, dark-blue jacket, short-sleeved black shirt, dark-blue pants and black boots made sense, though. It was light enough that, in an emergency over the water, it wouldn't sink you. Not that Valerie wanted to test it…

"I'm not sure what we're looking for either," she said to Alex. "I guess just anything unusual."

"I'd be happy to find *anything* at this point," Alex added.

As the SuperCopter's blades whipped around, they created a low, mesmerizing hum. Valerie scanned the clouds, remembering how she had inherited this mission in the first place. It started when she and Alex were called to Commander Kellie's planning room.

▲ ▲ ▲

Valerie Rivera and Alex Taylor sat across from their commander; their backs were straight and they listened intently. Valerie treasured the moment. She loved the importance of being sent on a mission, launched into a world of adventure.

Commander Kellie was sitting up straight, too. Her dark hair was down, playing on her shoulders. Her confident, hazel eyes read the Superkids as they received their briefing. Valerie had her dark hair down also, trying her hardest to appear as regal as her commander. Valerie straightened the leg of her royal blue Superkid uniform, pulling at the cloth with her hand. One day she would be behind a desk like this, calling in her Superkids and briefing them. The thought excited Valerie. She knew it would be awhile—hey, she was only 11—but it would happen. Valerie bit her lip. She knew there was a lot of training ahead of her. She would have to work hard to prove herself suitable for a commander position. That's what made it hard sometimes. She wanted so much to prove herself and hear "well done, Superkid"…but she also didn't want to make a mistake by stepping out at the wrong moment—and falling flat on her face. She knew the time would come when she would have to just step out in faith…but Valerie wondered if she would be believing God strongly enough when that crucial time came. Her thoughts began to exhaust her.

"Three months," Commander Kellie was saying, holding up three fingers. "In three months we've lost three aircraft over the Pacific Ocean. And all three were lost in the same general area. We want to know why."

"What happened to the pilots?" Alex wondered.

Commander Kellie brushed a strand of hair behind her right ear. "They're fine—when their systems mysteriously died, they ejected. But the 'Copters sank. And when we swept the ocean floor for them, we found no evidence they were ever there in the first place."

"They disappeared?" Valerie asked.

"They disappeared."

"And you want *us* to go look for them?" Alex inquired.

"I do," the commander confirmed. "Paul, Missy and Rapper have already left for Christmas. It's up to you."

"We can do it," Valerie said with a smile. Her stomach tightened a little as her mind added, *I hope!*

Alex asked, "How do we know Val and I won't disappear, too?"

Commander Kellie smiled. "We're equipping you

with"—Commander Kellie held up two fingers this time—"two SuperCopters that have multiple safety measures. You'll have complete backup engine systems, long-range scanners and, if all else fails, ejectable pilot seats.

"Plus," Commander Kellie added, "we're going to pray right now."

Valerie and Alex stood, following their commander's lead. They grabbed hands as Commander Kellie prayed. "Father God, I thank You for Your unfailing love toward us. I send Valerie and Alex out today to find the answers I know You want us to find. I assign angels to protect them according to Psalm 91:11, and we rejoice, for Psalm 37:23 states that You order their steps. Because of Your protection, we believe that nothing—no evildoer, no work of the enemy, no shark—shall by any means hurt them…"

Valerie's right eye popped open. *Did she just say "shark"?*

▲ ▲ ▲

BOOM!

Valerie jolted the steering yoke back as the SuperCopter trembled.

"What was that?!" she asked Alex. "Where'd it come from?"

"I'm not sure," Alex replied quickly. "Our aircraft are the only energy sources on the—"

Alex's voice disappeared.

"Alex?" Valerie called. "Alex?" She slapped the viewscreen. Alex's digital image was gone.

Valerie looked at the radar. It was blank. In fact, *all* the lights on the main control board were blank. Valerie tensed. She had never seen a SuperCopter just "die." The rhythm of the blades was slowing down. Valerie swung a quarter turn in her pilot's chair. She popped open the clear plastic box covering the manual backup system switch. She knew that behind her, Alex was doing the same thing.

It won't be that easy to stop us! Valerie thought. She flicked the switch.

The click echoed in the cabin, but nothing happened. Valerie's eyes widened in disbelief. The SuperCopter's flight console was still blank—the vehicle had absolutely no power. There wasn't even a spark of electricity in the backup systems. So much for being equipped with extra security measures.

Valerie coasted, looking ahead at the vast expanse of dark blue ocean in front of her. She flicked the manual switch back and forth time and again to no avail. She slapped the aircraft's console. Her hands shook. She didn't want to give up. She tried button after button, switch after switch—anything for a sign of life. Nothing worked. She looked ahead at the ocean again. Without the hum of electronics, the cabin was oddly peaceful...but she knew at any moment the whole vehicle would slap into the water. It would become another lost aircraft.

Suddenly she remembered she was wearing her ComWatch, a short-range communications watch by Warren Technologies that she wore on her right arm. She popped it on. "Alex!" Valerie cried into the watch's tiny viewscreen.

Alex's face appeared, brushing on and off the screen as he shouted back, "Valerie! My controls are gone! My—umph!" Alex's ComWatch hit something and flipped off.

"Alex!" Valerie cried. He didn't answer.

For a brief pause, Valerie closed her brown eyes. She quickly prayed, "Jesus, I trust in You—You are my strength when I am weak." The Superkid ran her fingers along the seat's straps, verifying their tightness. With her left hand, she removed a small, silver cylinder from her shirt pocket.

With her right hand, she pulled the eject cord.

Shhhhwwwwooooommmmm! Like a rocket, Valerie shot straight up and out of the SuperCopter, the sweet, salty air rushing from her lungs. The wind rushed around her as the air pulled tears from her eyes. Her short, brown hair wrapped around her face. She inwardly thanked God that the eject system was gear-released—not reliant at all upon electricity. Suddenly she began to reverse direction toward the water below.

Fpppaaapppp! A small parachute popped out of the top of the chair. Valerie was jerked upward again, and a large metal ring from the base of the chair dropped off. Then she began to drift downward. Valerie opened her eyes. The ocean below rolled in wait. Ahead, Valerie watched her SuperCopter smack against the water and lean forward against the current. Her heart skipped a beat as she saw Alex's SuperCopter barrel into her own with a crash, creating an awkward heap. The sound of metal scraping was like thunder.

Valerie shouted Alex's name as she scanned the sky. *Surely he ejected,* she thought.

She was about to try her ComWatch again when the ocean met her flight boots faster than she had anticipated. At once, she was fully immersed in the bitter water. The ocean waves lapped over her body and face. She gasped as she found the pilot seat release and yanked it. The seat belt straps popped away and Valerie grabbed the seat. She could have left it on as a flotation device, but she preferred not to be confined. The parachute drifted down slowly and folded on the moving water.

Valerie looked at the marred mess ahead. The SuperCopters hadn't sunk yet…but they were on their way. If she were to save Alex, she didn't have much—

"Look out below!!"

Valerie's brown eyes shot up and caught a glimpse of Alex's feet as he came barreling down, nearly on top of her. Valerie screamed as he splashed like a cannonball. She reached forward to grab him and was nearly pulled under the cold water herself. Alex freed himself from his chair, too. He kicked as he threw his falling parachute aside.

"Alex!" Valerie shouted. "Thank God you—"

"I don't ever, ever, *ever,* want to do that again." Alex interrupted. Valerie let out a burst of laughter. She couldn't help herself. "You made a pretty good cannonball," she jabbed.

"What happened anyway?" he asked.

"I don't know," Valerie replied. "The 'Copters just lost all power—even the backup systems."

"Did I mention I don't *ever* want to be a human cannonball again?" Alex asked.

Valerie nodded.

"Sharks, you stay away from me in the Name of Jesus!" Alex shouted. He felt his front pocket. He looked down at it. It was empty. "Please tell me you didn't lose your emergency beacon, too."

Valerie lifted her left hand. It was still clenched around the silver cylinder. Alex smiled.

"Thank You, Jesus," he said. Then, "Did you activate it yet?"

Valerie glanced toward the sinking SuperCopters.

Alex ran his dark hand down his face. "Please *nooo...*" he whined.

"Alex, if I press this beacon, we'll never find out what happened to our SuperCopters—or the others that disappeared. Remember our mission?"

Alex looked over his shoulder at the sinking aircraft.

"How are we going to investigate?" he asked.

"Think about this," Valerie prodded. "Our radars showed there were no other aircraft around. But they didn't scan *beneath* the ocean's surface."

"Who *would* scan down there?" Alex asked, sounding slightly irritated.

"Exactly," Valerie pointed out. "Down there is whatever it was that disabled us."

"So how do we get *down there?*"

"We have emergency scuba gear in the SuperCopters."

"The SuperCopters have sunk!"

Valerie glanced over at the sinking vessels. The water around them was bubbling. "Not yet they haven't."

Alex hesitated. "OK, but you know if we're beneath the surface, we can't use the beacon. Too much aquatic distortion."

"I just want to look for a clue," Valerie explained. "We can use the beacon when we get back up to the surface. We'll just look for one clue," she reassured her friend.

Alex let out a short breath. "You're the boss."

Valerie's brown eyes darted to Alex's. "That's not why I'm doing this. I'm not trying to prove anything."

Alex shrugged his shoulders. "It was just an expression..."

Valerie put the beacon in her belt. She bit her bottom lip and nodded.

▲ ▲ ▲

Valerie coughed as she came up for air inside the sinking SuperCopter. Her limbs felt weak. She and Alex swam all the way over to the SuperCopters and then dived under the water to get inside. Alex went into his craft, Valerie into hers. A pocket of air was inside the angled hull and

Valerie was thanking God for it. She took a huge gulp, but found it hard to hold for long. She let it out trying to relax herself, and took another. Then with all her strength, she pulled herself down to the storage drawer that held the emergency scuba gear. She tugged at the handle and her hand slipped. Her elbow flew back in slow motion and hit a bar. She lost half a mouthful of air. She swam back up to the air pocket.

Once again, Valerie gasped for air. She began to wonder if this was the best idea. It wasn't fun being out of breath. Alex had said he didn't want to be a human cannonball again—that was nothing compared to this. Soon the air pocket would be gone and she would either have her gear on, or she would sink with the SuperCopter. And what about Alex? Valerie wondered if splitting up really had been the best idea. What if he needed help? Maybe she'd made a mistake. Valerie closed her eyes. In her mind, she quoted Psalm 46:1, *God is my refuge and strength, an ever present help in trouble.* Valerie dove down again.

With a fresh breath of air, Valerie grabbed the drawer again and tugged. Her brown hair was swirling around in the water and getting in her way. She tugged harder. The drawer suddenly popped open—Valerie could hear it. The gear inside floated out. Valerie grabbed it and swam up for another breath. When she got to the pocket, it was nearly gone. The air was quickly being replaced with seeping water. Valerie could feel sudden motion as the aircraft was pulled down by gravity. Taking her last breath, Valerie fumbled with the scuba gear. The salt water burned her eyes.

Why did she ever decide to do such a ludicrous thing? Why didn't she just push the beacon and wait for help? What was she trying to prove? And where was Alex?

Valerie pulled the pack around in her hands. She couldn't tell the top from the bottom. One of the flippers sailed away from her. She looked up. She was sure the air pocket was gone. She glanced at the door as her lungs burned. She didn't have enough time to swim out and to the surface. The SuperCopter was sinking with her inside! What was she thinking?!

Her ears popped as the aircraft sailed down, carrying her with it.

A thousand thoughts barraged her mind when suddenly, as the Holy Spirit touched her heart, only one thought surfaced—Jesus! Jesus!

To Valerie's surprise, the pack unrolled and Valerie saw the face mask. She grabbed it and shoved it on her face. The water in her mask was spit out automatically—a miracle of advanced technology.

Whoosh! At once a stream of oxygen shot into her face, her lips opening involuntarily. Valerie sucked the air in like honey. As she stayed still for a moment, her lungs stopped burning. Without wasting time, the Superkid was finally able to locate the straps to the mask. She tightened it around her head, covering her ears with the soft rubber. She pulled the pack around her back. Grabbing the runaway flipper, she clumsily tightened them around her feet. When she looked up, she screamed.

Alex grabbed her arm and pulled her out of the twisted doorway. He kicked his flippers together and they ignited into a burst of bubbles. In seconds, the pair sailed clear of the sunken vessels. The melded SuperCopters crunched against the ocean floor, sending a rumble across the ocean.

Alex kicked his flippers together again and the motors inside came to a halt. Silently, the Superkids viewed the lifeless SuperCopters.

"Thank you," Valerie said to her friend.

"You're welcome," Alex transmitted back, his voice crackling in Valerie's ear.

2
The Coral Ship

"SHARK!"

Valerie's stomach turned as she spotted the great white shark heading in their direction. Both Superkids kicked their feet together and their flippers exploded into a burst of bubbles. Together they sailed quickly away, but the animal didn't give up. Valerie could see the hunger in his eyes…his movements.

"Where do we go?" Alex called to Valerie from his underwater headgear.

Valerie scanned the ocean expanse. They could go back to their crumpled SuperCopters or—

"There!" Valerie headed to the left. Alex was right behind her. Their motorized flippers were fast, but the shark was fast, too. For every foot they gained, the shark gained two.

"Go! Go! Go! Go!" Alex shouted.

"I'm going!" Valerie replied, angling her toes out. Ahead she spotted a huge, rocky expanse of coral. There was more than one nook and cranny in it—Valerie was sure she and Alex could fit in one of the larger ones.

Zzzzoooooommmmmm... The Superkids rocketed forward, the hungry great white at their heels. The shark snapped and Alex dove under Valerie, coming back up in front of her. The bubbles from his flippers clouded her view.

"I can't see!" she shouted. Alex angled to the right.

The shark nipped at Valerie, but she rolled right just in time.

"There!" Valerie shouted, pointing to a cave in the coral. "Go there!"

Alex dove down and disappeared into the cave seconds before Valerie joined at his side. The shark attempted to follow, but the Superkids were a step ahead of him. They both grabbed onto nubs in the hard rock surface and threw their feet toward the entrance. Their bubble-spitting flippers shot the shark with an irritating barrage of bubble clouds—he couldn't avoid it. After a few moments of trying bites at different angles, the annoyed shark retreated.

When it appeared safe, Valerie and Alex kicked their heels together, stopping the motors inside.

Valerie caught her breath. "I don't like sharks," she said, stating the obvious.

"Especially hungry ones," Alex added, breathing heavily.

For a moment, they rested in silence. Valerie would have liked to rest longer, but she knew their time was limited.

"Is this coral?" Alex asked. Valerie touched the surface. It was rough and hard.

"Out here? I don't know," she responded. "I've never touched coral before, but I think it's supposed to be soft when it's alive."

"Maybe it's just a gigantic, dead mound," Alex said.

Valerie added, "Alex, I'm really sorry about this."

Alex turned to look at her, his face barely distinguishable behind his face mask in the dark cave. "This isn't your fault, Valerie," he said. "Living for Jesus doesn't mean Satan leaves you alone. It just means you have to trust in God's protection. He always has a way to deliver you. Remember the story of Shadrach, Meshach and Abednego? Before they were cast into the fiery furnace, they said to King Nebuchadnezzer, 'Our God whom we serve is able to deliver us.'"

Valerie nodded. He was right. Suddenly Alex chuckled.

"What?" Valerie wondered aloud.

"It's just…you're usually the one giving *me* spiritual advice."

His statement made Valerie smile. "Well, let's take one last—"

Suddenly the coral began vibrating.

"What's going on?" Alex said cautiously.

"It's…moving," Valerie stated.

"Dead coral doesn't move," Alex pointed out. "And when it's alive, it just grows—usually less than an inch a year."

"Well, this coral is moving!" Valerie said. "Let's get out—"

Shoooooooooooommmmmmmmm!!!!! With a sudden gust of pressure, Valerie and Alex were tossed from the cave, head over heels. About 30 feet from the cave, they straightened themselves out enough to get their bearings. Valerie looked ahead at the coral.

"The coral is *moving!"* she stated again, not exactly sure what else to say.

Alex responded, "Val, I don't think that's coral."

"Then what is it?"

"How about a ship."

"A ship?"

"Could be. And that cave—one of its engines."

Valerie bit her lip. He was right. He *had* to be right. What other explanation was there? It did *sort of* look like a ship—saucer-shaped, camouflaged with the rocky, coral-looking substance. It was nearly the size of a three-story building. Suddenly light shot out all around the coral—from oddly placed windows, large and small.

"That's *definitely* a ship," Valerie stated. The coral ship smoothly moved forward over the ocean floor. It was heading straight for the SuperCopters.

Valerie kicked her heels together and launched forward. Alex was close behind. Careful to stay away from the windows, Valerie zipped along the top of the ship. As she moved in closer, she angled her feet down to slow her speed. The ship sure looked like coral, but as Valerie studied it up close, she could see thin, straight grooves in its surface. *Somewhere,* she thought, *this ship opens up.*

"Well, I'd say this is a pretty good clue," Alex said, sounding nervous. "Should we go back and report this?"

Valerie looked ahead at the crumpled SuperCopters.

"We don't have much air left," Alex explained. "Maybe half an hour."

"We've still got some time," Valerie countered.

Alex zipped around in front of her. Even through the glass of both face masks, Valerie could see he was genuinely concerned. "We need to use wisdom while in God's protection," he reminded her.

Valerie looked over Alex's shoulder at the SuperCopters again. In moments they would be upon them.

"OK," Valerie said. "Let me have 15 more minutes. When my time's up, we'll go to the surface and alert Superkid Academy."

Alex looked at her warily. Valerie reached down to her belt and pulled out the silver cylinder—the alert beacon. She placed it in Alex's hand with the words, "Fifteen minutes."

Alex nodded. "What's next then?"

Valerie angled her head toward the SuperCopter wreckage. "Follow me."

▲ ▲ ▲

Valerie and Alex had zipped over to the SuperCopters. They crouched down behind them, watching the ominous ship crawl along the ocean floor. Valerie could feel the ocean water swirling around her as it drew nearer. Time was passing quickly and Valerie knew Alex would say something soon. He was right about using God's wisdom, but Valerie longed to get that "one last detail" before returning to the surface. She was stepping out, hoping she wasn't making a mistake. It was hard sometimes "not knowing." Was she doing the right thing or not? She prayed as she went, asking the Holy Spirit for guidance, but she was moving so fast she wondered if she was really listening for His direction.

The soft roar of machinery pressed through the ocean water as the coral ship moved in. From the corner of her eye,

Valerie glanced at Alex. He was still, struck with interest.

The ship drew closer.

Valerie and Alex stayed put, hiding behind their fallen aircraft. Valerie was beginning to wonder if the coral ship was going to stop. It didn't. Sailing about 20 feet above the sandy, ocean floor, the coral ship kept moving—right over the SuperCopters, right over the Superkids.

Valerie gulped as it cast a dark shadow over her and Alex. Then it stopped, and the engines died down.

"I think I've seen enough," Alex whispered, looking up. "Let's get out of here."

"But what's it doing?" Valerie whispered back.

BANG!

Valerie's heart jumped.

A sudden blast of light showered them as double doors slid open on the belly of the ship.

"I think you're right," Valerie said to Alex. "It's time to get out of here."

Wwwuuuuuummmmmmmmm...

Not wasting any time, Valerie and Alex kicked their feet together. Bubbles exploded and they rocketed away. Suddenly Valerie heard Alex shout, "No!"

Valerie kicked her feet together and came to a quick stop. "What?" she asked.

Alex was pointing in the direction of the SuperCopters. The aircraft were being pulled up into the coral ship, slowly disappearing into the belly. Alex kicked his feet together again and headed back toward the SuperCopters.

"What are you doing?!" Valerie demanded.

"The beacon!" Alex shouted. "It just popped off my belt and is being pulled into the ship with the SuperCopters!"

Valerie saw it shooting through the water, straight toward the opening. "The ship must be using some kind of magnetic field to get the SuperCopters!" she shouted. "The beacon got caught in it!" Valerie launched after Alex. They had to get the beacon—it was their only way to call Superkid Academy.

Alex was several lengths ahead of Valerie. "Almost have it!" he shouted.

"Get it—get it!" Valerie chimed in.

"Got it!" Alex exclaimed, his fist wrapping around the silver cylinder.

Valerie came to a halt. "Excellent!"

"Wait!

"What?!"

"It's got *me!"*

Valerie's brown eyes grew wide as she watched Alex, with the beacon in hand, being pulled up with the

SuperCopters. He kicked his heels together, but the motorized flippers didn't do any good. The magnetic field was stronger than he was. The SuperCopters were nearly all the way inside the coral ship

"I'm coming!" Valerie cried. "Don't let go!"

Kicking her heels together again, Valerie shot forward, determined. She reached Alex and grabbed his waist.

"Together, on three," she said, "we kick and go full blast against the field."

"All right!" Alex agreed.

"One," Valerie counted, "two, thr—"

BOOM! The doors beneath them shut. The lights went out. Valerie shuddered. They were *inside* the coral ship.

▲ ▲ ▲

All Valerie could hear was Alex's nervous breathing.

Then the booming started. Loud echoes of slamming and banging, reverberating through the water. Valerie heard herself quote verses from Psalm 23 on reflex. When she was younger and afraid of the dark, her mother would quote them to her again and again to help her sleep. "Even though I walk through the valley of the shadow of death, I will fear no evil, for you are with me; your rod and your staff, they comfort me."

Then the sound of running water began. No—it was draining water…draining from all around her. As it drained, Valerie felt her feet touch solid ground.

Then hissing—screaming from all sides—like air being forced into a tire by pressure. A sudden wind against Valerie's body made it hard for her to stay standing. Then stillness.

"We're dry," Alex said, piercing the silence. Valerie touched her flight jacket. Alex was right. She was *completely* dry. Valerie pulled her mask away from her face, still leaving it fastened around her head. She took a short breath.

"Alex, I can breathe—without my face mask on," she told her friend. She heard him lift his face mask.

"Wherever we are, it's airtight," he said. Valerie pulled her face mask completely off.

"Can you see anything?" Valerie asked.

Alex didn't respond.

"I can't see your head shaking," Valerie said.

Alex chuckled nervously. "No," he said. "I can't see anything."

FOOOOOMMMM! Bright lights shattered the darkness, forcing Valerie and Alex to squeeze their eyes tight. Valerie tried to open hers, but the sudden light was almost unbearable. She squinted. The room was blurred as her eyes tried to focus. She could see something…some *big* figure coming toward her. And it appeared to have… *fire* flying from its hands…

3
Hints of Treasure

Valerie's vision cleared just in time for her to grab Alex's arm and dodge to the left. The dodge turned into more of a flop as they both rolled and ended up on their backs. The figure that approached them—a flat-metal, bare-bones robot—was holding a large, sparking, laser ray. The simple-minded taskbot completely ignored them. It pressed the laser against a panel on the tangled SuperCopters and melted away the hinges. When the panel dropped to the floor it was scooped up by another, similar-looking taskbot. The second computer-brained robot deposited the panel and some other parts on a conveyor belt that slid out of the room. One by one, the SuperCopter's parts disappeared into a big, black, squared hole in the wall.

"Once again I'm a human cannonball," Alex noted before he sat up and asked, "Why are they taking apart the SuperCopters?"

"They're building something?" Valerie said as more of a question than a statement.

Valerie was sitting up now, too. The room glowed

from long, yellowish light strips in the ceiling. Except for the SuperCopters, the conveyor belt and the taskbots, the room was empty. The ceiling and floor were constructed of metal. This room lacked any windows. On the far side, Valerie spotted a short series of metal stairs leading to a large, rounded door with a porthole window in the top center.

"Well, our 15 minutes are up," Alex noted. "What do you say we return to the surface?"

Valerie shot him a look with her eyebrows raised. "Very funny."

"Heh, heh," Alex offered, clearly indicating he wasn't joking.

Valerie reached down and tugged the flippers off her feet. Her flight boots were still on her feet, making her flight outfit complete. She popped open the buttons on the dark blue jacket. "I wonder what they're building with all these pieces…"

Alex took off his flippers, too. The taskbot removed an electronic card from the SuperCopter and its partner placed it on the belt. Valerie focused on the conveyor belt.

"OK," Valerie said after a long breath, "I'm thinking I'd really like to find out what they're building."

"You're kidding?!" Alex asked. Then he added, "Well,

we might as well. Until we find a way to communicate with Superkid Academy, we have nothing better to do."

"That's the spirit," Valerie cheered. The Superkids stood up.

Valerie continued, "We need to be careful to stay hidden. We have no idea how many thugs could be on the other side of that door." Valerie paused as she looked at the door. Then, "Let's do our best to find out who's doing this, what they're building and how we can alert Commander Kellie."

"Sounds like a plan to me," Alex offered.

"We can speed our efforts by splitting up and talking on our ComWatches. While one of us is looking for a way to call the Academy, the other can find out what they're building on the other side of that belt." Valerie tapped her ComWatch. It blinked for a second, but then fizzled. "Well, maybe we won't communicate by ComWatch."

Alex tried his ComWatch, but it fizzled, too. He twisted his lip and then entered the dry SuperCopters. He returned moments later with two more ComWatches. "There was a spare in each 'Copter," he said, checking one out as he handed it to Valerie. "They haven't been affected."

"Excellent," Valerie complimented, tossing her old ComWatch into the wreckage. She put the new one on her wrist. In an instant, she'd linked up with Alex's Com-Watch and could see his face on the screen. She smiled and then put the watch in standby mode. "So you want to take the door or the conveyor belt?" she asked.

Alex nodded toward the conveyor belt. "I'm going to steer away from the thugs. I'll go that way," he said.

"Let's pray," Valerie suggested, grabbing Alex's hand. Then she began, "Dear Father God, we thank You for protecting us. You have in the past and we know according to Hebrews 13:8 that You're the same yesterday, today and forever. We stand in agreement, knowing You're here with us. Thank You that You said in Proverbs 3:6 that You would make our paths straight when we acknowledge You. In Jesus' Name, amen."

Alex repeated Valerie's "amen." Valerie gave her friend a few pats on the back and they separated. As Valerie approached the door, she watched Alex investigate the conveyor belt. He shrugged his shoulders and, after peering into the black hole, stepped onto the belt himself and waved "goodbye." Valerie waved back. She made her way up the metal stairs embossed with crisscrosses. At the top of the stairway she pressed a button. The door slid open with a light clanking sound. Valerie hid around the corner until she was certain there was no one in the hallway on the other side. After she stepped through, the door closed behind her.

The hallway ahead was a long stretch of nondescript metal and doors, highlighted by a long, muted ceiling light. Valerie almost went down the hall, door by door, but decided against it. Each one had a small electronic "open" button at its side, lit in red—a universal signal that they were locked tight. The good news was that at the end of the hall there was a ladder leading straight up. She knew she was in the belly of the ship and, based on her experience, the communication controls were sure to be near the top. She headed up the ladder, careful to tread lightly.

At the top of the ladder, Valerie poked her head up through the ceiling and into the hallway. This one was nearly identical to the last except it was longer and had many more hallways leading off it. *Welcome to Maze 101!* she thought, twisting her lip. The good news was, at least the halls were empty. She pulled herself up onto the floor. The low-ceilinged hallway was silent except for the humming of the ship. At the far end was another ladder heading up. Valerie imagined that the ship couldn't have too many floors—three or four at the most. But it had enough width to make each floor confusing, only making sense to a seasoned veteran. Slowly, staying close to the cold wall,

Valerie made her way down the hall.

The first three doors on Valerie's left *and* right were locked and had no windows. She continued on. With each step, the Superkid could hear her heart beating in her ears. She wondered what size crew was on the vessel. Fifty? A hundred? More? At any moment, someone could turn the corner and spot her. Valerie's only consolation was that the floors were metal, so she was sure to hear them coming—unless they wore bunny slippers. Not likely.

All the intersections looked entirely nondescript. Just halls and locked doors, probably leading to staff quarters, bathrooms, boiler rooms and utility closets. She stayed in the main hall so she wouldn't get lost. At the end of the corridor, Valerie had three choices: up another ladder, down another hall or into a large open room. Valerie looked into the room to her right. It was a beautiful room, dressed in tapestries with golden weaves. In the center was a long, polished table with at least 20 chairs. The floor, instead of metal, was wooden, partially covered in a wide, mauve and hunter green rug. Along the back wall was a bookcase filled with fragile china pieces—plates and bowls and saucers and cups. Tall, crystal goblets adorned the top of the cabinet.

On the other side of the room was a small door with a

window, which Valerie guessed led to the kitchen. Directly opposite Valerie, on the other side of the table, was a series of dark slabs of glass. Valerie couldn't figure out their purpose. The room was beautiful, but Valerie turned away from it. She was still on a mission. She climbed up the ladder.

Another level of corridor and intersections made Valerie shake her head. *How many of these can there be?* Valerie knew it was a big ship—a *huge* ship. But she was hoping for *something* notable. Valerie pulled herself to the next level and began down the corridor. When her foot caught a bolt, she nearly fell forward and her foot slapped against the metal as she caught herself. Valerie froze. *Did anyone hear that?* Nothing happened. No one showed up yelling, "Hey!" Suddenly Valerie found herself thinking about the other extreme: What if there weren't 50, 75 or 100 in the crew? What if the crew was all robots run by an onshore remote? But, then, why have a dining room?

Just for kicks, Valerie pushed the red-lit button by the first door. It was locked. Surprise, surprise. The next five doors in the hallway were locked, too. At the far end "T" intersection, this time leading down two hallways, Valerie spotted a wheeled cart. On the top was a series of rolled-up papers, sitting atop one another, each one tied with a thin, purple ribbon. An elegant red cloth was draped over the cart. Valerie was about to open one of the paper scrolls when she heard the unmistakable echo of footsteps. Someone was coming…from the hallway above. Valerie looked up and saw a thick shoe hit the top rung of the ladder. A *large* thick shoe. She had to get out of there *fast.*

Valerie looked down each hall. It was too far to run to make it around a corner, and too loud. She could try the doors, but if she hit more than one locked one, she'd be caught for sure. Valerie looked down at the cart. It was pretty big. And it was covered. The Superkid yanked the red cloth aside. The cart was empty! She flipped the cloth up and stuffed herself inside in a matter of seconds.

Please go! Please go! Please go! she hoped. The feet made their way down the ladder and clomped onto the floor. Valerie stayed frozen. She tilted her head to see out between the folds of the red cloth. The feet were attached to gray, baggy pants, stained with age. The feet and legs stopped in front of the cart. The rolls of paper rustled. The feet and legs walked around the cart. Valerie balled her right fist—*just let him try and pull up the cloth.* But he never did. Instead, the cart began rolling. Valerie gulped. The wheels squealed with every rotation, bumping on the decorative, crisscross indentations in the metal floor.

The jarring caused a lock of Valerie's brown hair to fall into her face. It tickled her nose and made her want to scratch. She found herself holding her breath. For a moment, the cart stopped. The feet and legs walked around the cart. She heard a click, then the sliding of a door. Valerie was rolled over a bumpy threshold and into a room. The cart stopped. The feet and legs then walked away, echoing down the corridor. After they were gone, she waited at least five more minutes, catching her breath and making sure they didn't come right back. Then she pushed the red cloth aside.

Valerie squeezed her way out of the cart. This room was even more beautiful than the dining room. It was a bedroom with plush, dark carpeting. A king-sized bed with purple velvet covers spilled into the room. On a mahogany bed stand sat an electronic tablet version of *Treasure Island* by Robert Louis Stevenson and a thick, paper book labeled, *Captain's Log.* Valerie spun around and looked at the open door, thinking she had heard something in the corridor. But it was quiet.

A small door by a wide dresser with a mirror led to a bathroom—or "head," as they called it on a ship. Another door on the other side of the dresser was closed, but Valerie guessed it led to a closet. Valerie turned her attention back to the cart and the paper rolls on top. Carefully she picked one up and untied the purple ribbon. She glanced down the hall to be sure no one had heard the paper crinkle. And then she opened it.

Inside, turquoise lines mapped out a detailed schematic of the coral ship. A label at the top revealed it was for "Level 4." Valerie realized Level 4 was most likely the top level of the ship when she spied a label reading "MCR"—the Main Control Room. Another label popped out at her, too. It was labeled "SENTRY" and pointed to a small X…sitting inside "BAY." Valerie wondered if the *Sentry* was a small ship within this larger one. She knew there had to be at least one smaller, scout boat on board…it could be her and Alex's ticket to freedom. After making a mental note about its location from the main corridor, she rolled the sheet back up. She then gently retied the ribbon around the schematic and set it back in place.

She looked out at the hallway again. No one.

Quietly, Valerie walked over to the journal. She picked it up. It felt funny holding a paper book in her hands; she hadn't for years. Most books and tablets were available in electronic versions now…even Valerie's pocket Bible was on a small, electronic pad.

Valerie opened the log to the middle. The script was

smooth and elegant, written in thin, black ink. She read:

but what does it matter? Fresh cuisine is the least of my concerns.

Another today—a zf42 Perry-Flyer. I was especially interested in this one as it has a proprietary airplosion intake system. Quite the find. Perfect for my endeavors. At this rate, I ought to have my treasure by my early 40s. History will remember me. For I shall be known around the globe as the greatest treasure hunter that ever lived. Aye, the greatest pirate! I shall

Valerie slammed the book shut and jumped when she heard the voice. She nearly screamed, but swallowed her speech instead. She whirled around, ready to defend herself…but no one was there.

"It's me!" the voice said. Valerie turned to her Com-Watch. Her heart stopped pounding so fast when she realized it was just her friend calling her.

"Hey," she said, "you surprised me. You find anything?"

"Not really," Alex replied. "Just a bunch of junk. Literally. I think I've stumbled onto some kind of junkyard or something. There are mounds of ship parts everywhere."

"I found a journal," Valerie stated, turning back around to look at it. "It talks about pirates and treasure. Do you think they might be building some kind of treasure-hunting technology?"

In the view screen of the ComWatch, Valerie could see Alex shrug his shoulders. "Could be," he said. "It's the best theory yet."

Next, Valerie told Alex about the scrolled maps she'd found. She described the general layout of Level 4 and she told him about the area marked "BAY" and "SENTRY."

"It might be some sort of small boat," Valerie noted. "Maybe our ticket out of here."

"I'll check it out next," Alex promised, "unless you get there fir—"

"HEY!"

Valerie spun on her heels, instinctively slapping off her ComWatch connection. She raised her arms to protect herself like she had been taught in the Superkid Academy training courses.

Before her stood the familiar, thick feet and legs—only this time, she saw the mammoth body to which they were connected. It was at least 7-feet tall and male. His frame wasn't fat, but thick—from head to toe. He didn't even look like he had a neck. His head was bald and his face, though frowning at the moment, had a youthful look. A big nose and a few missing teeth testified to a history of brawls…all of which he'd probably won. He wore a simple, brown shirt, not quite covering his belly. His gray pants hung loosely off his knees. Valerie noticed all of this as the lug lurched forward. She turned around to escape, but before she could jump away, he threw his arms around her, making her defenseless. His grip was as tight as chain links wrapped around her torso. She screamed and he chuckled.

Jesus! she prayed, *You are my Deliverer!*

4
Pirates of Old

Valerie might have considered trying to make a run for it if her feet had been touching the floor. But instead, she hung defenseless in the big ogre's arms. She tried kicking at one point, but stopped when she realized she was hurting herself more than she was hurting him. She tried talking to him, but he never talked back. He just marched forward, humming some sailor's ballad. She felt like a prize he was getting ready to show off.

Their long, slow journey through the vessel ended when they passed through the door to the bridge. Most of the hallways had looked similar, but the bridge was entirely different.

A wide band of windows encircled half the room, providing a breathtaking view of the ocean. Dark shades of blue danced around the windows, highlighted by floodlights on the ship's bow. Inside, colored lights blinked and map screens detailed the topography of the ocean floor. A plush, leather chair with a high back hid someone at the main controls. It began to turn as Valerie and her captor drew closer. Like a rag doll, Valerie was tossed to the ground. Her knees crunched under her. She threw her hands to the cold, metal floor to keep her face from hitting.

"Ophus found her," she heard the ogre say, his voice a deep, slow drawl.

Valerie, down on her hands and knees, raised her head slowly. Her brown hair hung in front of her eyes.

She saw his boots first. They stood firm—shiny, black boots, slightly separated, with the toes pointing outward. Her gaze drifted up to his baggy, black-velvet trousers. Thin, Caucasian hands wrapped around each side of his shiny black belt. His shirt was dark purple, accented on every edge with ruffles. His long, thick beard was full of curly locks and just as jet black as his belt, pants and boots. Hanging from his neck was golden jewelry and a thin, leather rope with a plastic card on the end. His face was long and thin with a slender, down-turned nose. His eyes were like coal, his ears pierced with golden loops. His head was adorned with a black, three-cornered hat, rimmed in gold. A deep violet plume jutted out from the back, making him look like he'd just stepped out of the *Treasure Island* book Valerie had seen on what she assumed was his night-stand. For that reason, she wasn't all that surprised when an olive-feathered parrot landed on his shoulder, its wings folding against its body. Quite honestly, to Valerie, he looked ridiculous. He was straight out of a comic book or movie—way too eccentric to take too seriously. But the scowl on his face let Valerie know he was *very* serious…and not at all pleased with her intrusion.

"What are you doing aboard my zhip?" the man asked. His accent was thick and French.

Valerie moved her mouth to speak, but nothing came out. She rolled back onto her toes, but didn't raise to a stance.

"Do you know who I am?" he demanded. His dark eyebrows hid the top of his eyelids.

Valerie said the first name that came to mind. "Captain Hook?"

The man didn't miss a beat. "Ha-ha. Like I have never heard zat one before. But I am not a myth. I am very real—I assure you of zat. Guess again."

Guess again?

Valerie stood up slowly, suppressing the urge to guess "Cap'n Crunch." Instead, she said, "Sir, I don't know who—"

"I am Captain Jean-Luc Pierre Leblanc, ze zird! My father was a pirate, my grandfather was a pirate and my great grandfather was…"—his face crinkled—"well, he was a grocer, but never mind zat!"

Valerie's forehead wrinkled. *Is this guy for real?*

"Perhaps you have heard of me," he prompted as he started to pace in front of her. "I was ze first to compu-raid ze Nautical Bank and Trust. I checkmated Robbie ze Goon out of his estate in a skilled game of chess. I am a creator of technologies! Distributor of power! Historian of unmarred history! I am Captain Jean-Luc Pierre Leblanc, ze zird!"

Valerie slightly shrugged her shoulders. The captain tipped his head.

"But zen again," he continued, "you must know *zumthing* about me…after all, you are aboard my zhip." He stopped pacing and leaned his long, thin face into Valerie's. "Zo who are you, little girl?"

Valerie gulped, but wasn't afraid to answer. "I am Valerie Rivera, a Superkid. And I am on a mission to find who's been crashing and stealing our aircraft."

Captain Leblanc's coal-colored eyes lit up. "Ah! Zo you *have* heard of me! Yes—I am ze one who has captured your aircraft…as well as many others. Zo, you have found me…too bad for you."

"Why is that too bad?"

Leblanc smirked. "I can hardly let you live with ze knowledge of where I have been hiding, can I? No, zat would not go over well for me and my business."

"What business?" Valerie quizzed, not missing a beat.

"*My* business," Leblanc responded, not giving an inch.

Valerie looked at the gold chains around the captain's neck, the rich clothing he displayed so proudly. He was a thief and proud of it. And pride, Valerie remembered from Proverbs 16:18, always leads to destruction. Leblanc obviously didn't know about Alex or he would have said something. His robots had dismantled the SuperCopters so fast, he probably never even realized the tangled mass of metal was more than one vessel. Valerie knew that even though her life was being threatened, she had the upper hand. She had a hidden companion aboard. Now she just had to buy time. And that would be easy—since she was up against a man of pride.

"So you have a successful business?" Valerie asked.

Captain Leblanc smiled. "Undisputedly."

"Where's your crew?" Valerie wondered.

Leblanc nodded at the big lug who'd captured Valerie. "You have already met Ophus," he said. "Zat is my crew."

"You two run this whole ship—this whole operation—alone?"

"I prefer ze term 'zingle-handedly,' but yes. Impressed?"

Valerie raised her eyebrows. "Impressed that two

grown men hide under the ocean and steal aircraft like cowards? Not really."

Leblanc blinked, but didn't recoil. Valerie wasn't surprised—hey, he was a pirate.

"Join me for dinner," he offered. "Ze least I can do is give you a good last zupper."

Valerie gulped. "Last supper?"

"Aye," the pirate continued, "for ze next eight or nine hours, we will be going deeper to keep our location zecret. Zen, overnight our zhip will rise to ze zurface—far away from our present position. Finally, before breakfast, you will walk ze plank."

Valerie could hardly believe her ears. "Walk the plank?" she echoed.

"It is ze way of ze pirates," Leblanc said simply. Then he leaned into her face, bobbed his thick, black eyebrows and said, "You don't mind zharks, do you?"

"My God will protect me!" Valerie snapped back.

"You mean like He has protected you zo far?" Leblanc asked.

Valerie just stared back at her captor, speechless.

"Don't bother trying to find me yet," Valerie said to

Alex via her ComWatch. Alex's face peered back at her with a note of concern. "Really—I'm all right," she continued. "He put me in a decent room, even if there is a keycode to get in the door. I just want to wait until after supper. The captain wants me to eat with him and he may tell me what's going on." With Ophus standing guard outside the room, Valerie spoke in hushed tones. Leblanc had placed her in one of the ship's many extra bedrooms, "for her comfort." At least she had a bed, a bathroom and a small, circular window that looked out into the black, ocean depths.

"I found the *Sentry,*" Alex announced. "It's a fully operational speedboat. He probably uses it to get to land and back."

"Excellent," Valerie congratulated. Then, "So can we use it underwater?"

"Nope," Alex replied, "it's a surface boat only. But I'll keep a lookout for anything else useful."

Valerie thought for a moment. "The captain said we're going deeper before we rise to the surface tomorrow," she remembered. "If we have no choice, we may have to wait until then to take off in the *Sentry.*"

"There's a catch," Alex noted. "The *Sentry* is locked in place. We'll need an access card."

Valerie remembered the plastic card dangling around Leblanc's neck. "I think I know just where to find it," she said.

"Can you get it?" Alex asked.

"Maybe. But I might need your help."

"I'll find you tonight, sometime after supper."

"Good," Valerie responded. "I don't want to walk the plank."

"What?"

"It's a long story," Valerie explained, trying to smile.

Dinner took place in the dining room, which Valerie had already visited when she'd first boarded the coral ship. This time Ophus escorted her there, his big feet thumping behind her own. When they arrived, Valerie took a seat at the end of the long, polished table. Leblanc's vacant seat was on the opposite side—18 chairs away. Behind her was the bookcase filled with china plates, bowls, saucers and cups. Behind Leblanc's seat was a small door, which Ophus entered and exited as he brought items to the table. It was quite apparent Ophus would be serving them, not joining them.

Valerie gripped the slender water glass and took a

drink of crystal clear water. It tasted wonderful. The smell of roasting meat drifted from the kitchen and her stomach growled. It had been more than six hours since she'd last eaten anything. She was looking forward to a decent meal. Her thoughts drifted to Alex, who had to be just as hungry as she was. She made a mental note to let him know where the kitchen was so he could raid it later.

The thought of jumping up and running away crossed Valerie's mind, but she let it pass. She wanted to find out more. And this, it seemed, was the only way. Sure, she was stepping out into the unknown, but at least she still had the comfort of knowing Alex was out there somewhere. She looked over her shoulder at the dark slabs of glass covering the outer wall. She realized it wasn't the glass that was dark, but the ocean beyond. She was looking out windows…into a deep sea of nothingness.

When Valerie heard the squawk of Leblanc's parrot, she turned toward the door. The bird flew in and took a perch on a wooden banana stand near Leblanc's seat. Leblanc entered next. He looked the same as earlier. All purple and black, like a royal Captain Hook. He took his time walking to his seat. He stretched his back as Ophus pulled out his chair. Then he sat down. Valerie took another sip of the cool water.

"Zank you for joining me," the pirate said to Valerie. The Superkid set her water glass back down on the table. The clink of glass against varnished wood echoed in the room. Valerie didn't say a word.

"Now do not be rude," Leblanc said to her. "Common etiquette—even for pirates—is to be kind while being entertained on another's boat."

Valerie looked her captor in the eye. She could feel her body tensing. She didn't say it as an accusation, but rather as a fact: "You've kidnapped me and threatened to feed me to the sharks."

"Do not live in ze past or ze future, my dear. Live in ze present." The pirate threw his arms into the air as he said the words. "Now we are about to eat a hearty meal together. I zuggest you enjoy it, zince it will be your last."

Valerie gave him a cold stare. She had thought about playing it cool, but she knew she had to show her disapproval. If she didn't, he might guess something was up. After all, smiles and winks aren't generally the expected reactions from kidnapped victims.

Truth was, though, she was *a little* afraid. She didn't want to be. She knew 2 Timothy 1:7 says that fear doesn't come from God…but still her stomach felt tight. She struggled to bring her thoughts in line with God's promise:

He would protect her. He would rescue her. She could trust in Him. That's what she had been taught all her life. That is what she believed. That is what she wouldn't let go of…that is what she *couldn't* let go of…

Ophus trudged across the room and placed a china plate in front of Valerie. It had a big turkey leg on top, served with baked carrots in sweet juice on the side. It looked great. Valerie put her cloth napkin in her lap and waited for Leblanc to receive his meal. She let him begin eating first. Then she bowed her head and thanked God for her meal. Even if it came from an enemy, as far as Valerie was concerned, God was providing for her.

Valerie slipped her silver fork into the carrots and took a bite. They were delicious. She wasn't quite sure how to eat the turkey leg until she saw Leblanc wrap his hand around his and begin chomping. Valerie followed suit.

The room stayed relatively quiet until Leblanc's bird squawked, "Donga donna shoot! Donga donna shoot!"

"Zhut up," Leblanc said to the bird. It did. The pirate peered up at Valerie. "Ztupid bird always wants to greet our guests during dinner."

Valerie put down her finished turkey leg. "So are you going to tell me what this is all about?"

Leblanc wiped his mouth with his napkin. "I do

not mix business with dinner."

The room fell quiet again until Valerie asked, "So why did you become a pirate?"

Leblanc looked up from his meal and smiled warmly as he chewed. "I cannot zink of a greater profession."

"I can," Valerie countered before she caught herself.

Leblanc plopped his turkey leg down on his plate and rolled his eyes. He sat up straight in his chair and stared at Valerie. He wiped his hands on his cloth napkin and then stroked his curly, black beard with his slender fingers. "You really do not understand, do you?"

"I guess not," Valerie said, shrugging her shoulders.

"A pirate is zomeone who plunders ze zea. A pirate is an attacker! A man of real force—who overtakes other zhips without zeir consent."

"Oh." Valerie paused. *Yeah, right.*

"Piracy," he said the word carefully, "goes back zousands of years. It is not all hooks and peg legs and Long John Zilver. Zat is ze ztuff of books and legend."

Valerie glanced at Leblanc's parrot. He squawked at her.

"Aye, even parrots are of legend. Call me zentimental. But ze true pirates were people who ripped zrough ze oceans, taking what zey wanted. You have heard of Blackbeard?

He was zo treacherous, ze *world* feared him. You have heard of Great Pirate Roberts? He was zo powerful, ze government did not want to rustle him. How about Captain Kidd? He was originally employed to get rid of pirates... and zen he defected and gained possession of ze greatest amount of treasure ever. Zere were even a couple women pirates—Mary Read and Anne Bonny—who were as fierce and mean as any man."

Valerie looked at Leblanc, disbelieving. "But they all lived lives of sin and trouble. They couldn't trust anyone."

"Zat is ze price you pay," Leblanc admitted, waving his hand in the air.

"It's a costly one," Valerie noted. "What became of all these pirates?"

Leblanc ran his tongue across the inside of his bottom lip. Then he said, "Blackbeard was beheaded, Roberts was killed in battle, Kidd was hanged zree times—"

"Three times?"

"It did not work ze first two. And Anne and Mary… eh…one died in prison, ze other disappeared without a trace."

Good thing she had finished eating, because Valerie had lost her appetite. She sat back and questioned once again, "So what's the reason *you* became a pirate?"

"Because I, my dear, am zmarter zan zey were."

"Of course," Valerie wanted to say, but didn't.

"I have studied zeir victories and zeir failures. And I have discovered how to find treasure even Captain Kidd would admire. My only regret is zat I was not born zooner zo I could zhare ze zeas with zuch zcum." Leblanc leaned back himself and stared at Valerie across the shiny table, his deep-set eyes twinkling. "Zo what will you regret, Valerie? What will you regret about not zeeing ze day after tomorrow?"

Valerie studied the pirate and shook her head. "I have no regrets," she said. "My treasure is stored in heaven—Matthew 6:20 says so. If you were to feed me to the sharks, I'd go to a far better place. But it's not my time. I'm not afraid. God will protect me. I believe His Word."

The pirate touched his fingertips together as he stared at Valerie. The Superkid stared back, not saying anything more. As she looked at him, she thought about her dreams to one day be a commander herself. If her life were to end, she *would* regret not having become a commander. And what about growing up? Getting married? Having kids of her own? Valerie didn't know why she was suddenly hit with this barrage of thoughts, but it started her contemplating. She didn't want her life to end. She had to believe God. She had to.

Valerie's thoughts were jarred when Leblanc got up and walked to her end of the table. He looked into her eyes.

"Fine," he stated, "do not zhare your final regrets with me. But I know you have zem. I can zee it in your eyes." Then he held an open hand to her. "Well, come on," he said. "Dinner is over. And it is time for you to zee why I am zmarter zan ze rest. It is time for you to zee what zis is all about."

5
The Paralyzer

The windows were tall and wide, encompassing the entire wall of the room. They were similar to the glass slabs in the dining room, but much larger. Leblanc called this room the "observation room." When he turned on some outside spotlights, Valerie could finally, truly see the vast expanse of the ocean…miles and miles wide. Sure, she had seen it earlier from behind her diving mask, but from here—inside the coral ship—it appeared so much larger. She still didn't see any plants or swimming creatures—just a huge, peaceful, dark blue/midnight black void. Valerie looked up at Leblanc, who was standing beside her, silently watching. With his right hand, he was slowly rubbing the pendant of one of his golden necklaces. He was quiet. The majesty of the view had struck him, too.

Ophus was still in the kitchen, a few rooms away. Valerie could hear him cleaning dishes—a clatter here, a clatter there. Leblanc stayed quiet until his parrot flew into the room and landed on his shoulder squawking, "Donga donna shoot! Donga donna shoot!"—apparently they were the only "words" he could squawk.

"Ze grand zea," the pirate said, as if announcing its existence for the first time. "It is beautiful, yes?"

Valerie nodded. Then, softly, "It is."

"Pirates have dug under zis ocean for ages, zearching for hidden treasure. But zere is zo much zpace! You could zearch forever."

Valerie just nodded again, silently, still looking forward. As if it were breathing, tiny clouds of bubbles spit out from the coral ship at regular intervals. They created a soothing effect. Suddenly Leblanc slapped Valerie on her upper arm with the back of his hand.

"Aw—look at you look at ze ocean. You could have been a pirate. You could have zhown Mary or Anne a zing or two."

Valerie couldn't help but smile slightly. "So when are you going to tell me what it is you're doing out here?" she asked, taking a stab. "Are you looking for hidden treasure?"

Leblanc shook his head. He pulled off his black and gold hat and scratched his curly scalp. "Why would a man need to find *hidden* treasure when he can find *zunken* treasure?" he asked.

Valerie looked at Leblanc, searching for a clue in his eyes. She asked, "Aren't they the same?"

"To zome," the pirate responded nonchalantly. But then assertively, "but not to me."

For a long moment, his words hung in the air. Then he pointed out, "I have discovered zomething zey never did."

That was Valerie's cue. "What's that?"

Leblanc continued to look forward as he said, "I have discovered zat ze zame zea zat masks zunken treasure can mask ze pirate. Blackbeard, Captain Kidd, Mary Read, Anne Bonny—zey were all captured because zey came out of ze zea. Zey got on land—unfamiliar ground for pirates—and zey became defenseless."

"So you plan to stay at sea forever? It *is* beautiful," Valerie said, "but it's also lonely."

"Ze undersea paradise is hidden from ze world above. Here I can live life to its fullest. Here I can enjoy my treasure."

"Alone," Valerie added.

Leblanc twisted his lips. "Zat is right. Alone. I enjoy my treasure alone, but all ze treasure is mine—alone. Nobody takes a portion of ze bounty." He paused. "It is lonely at ze top…but worth it."

The pirate stared out the window again and let out a long, slow breath. "Treasure," he stated, sounding philosophical. "It has changed a lot over ze years. Treasure used to be gold and zilver and jewels," he waved his hand with each word. "Now it is technology—building ze bigger and better. Not in zize, but in concept."

Valerie put her hands on her hips and turned to face the pirate. "So is that what you're stealing aircraft for? Are you building some kind of bigger and better technology to search for sunken treasure?"

Leblanc threw his head back and laughed like a cartoon villain. "No, no!" he shouted. Then his voice trickled down. "Is zat what you zink?" He turned to Valerie. "You zink I am building zomething? No, my dear, I have already built it. But it is not technology to *find* zunken treasure. It is technology to *create* zunken treasure."

Valerie's dark brown eyebrows popped up. *Create sunken treasure?*

The pirate turned, his necklaces jerking sideways. "Follow me," he ordered. Then he walked out of the room. Valerie followed close behind.

▲ ▲ ▲

To Valerie's surprise, there was another level above the main control room—a level that could only be accessed with the card around Leblanc's neck. "My zecurity," Leblanc announced, tapping the plastic card with his index finger. "I am ze only one who has it and ze only one who grants access to zpecific areas of my zhip." His words confirmed to Valerie that the card was most probably the same key needed to free the *Sentry* ship that Alex had found and she had seen on the scrolls.

At the top of a short ladder, a metal panel opened in response to the sliding of Leblanc's security card. The pirate smiled and started up the rungs. Again, Valerie knew she could run away with a good head start, but then she wouldn't find out what was going on. Leblanc obviously knew this, which is why he didn't think twice about being the first one up the ladder. Valerie followed her tour guide.

The room they entered was wide and dimly lit. The floor was made of the same steel laid throughout the rest of the ship, but the ceiling was altogether different. It was domed, broad and low, and inconsistent in texture. It was the upper surface of the coral ship. Down the middle of the ceiling ran two long lines, intersecting at the center. The ceiling was obviously made so it could open, though now it was sealed tight. Effectively, when the ship surfaced, the ceiling could peel back. When it did, Valerie realized, she would be standing on the top deck.

Leblanc cleared his throat, begging for Valerie's

attention. He was standing on a small, raised platform, surrounded by a steel semicircle, forming a thin wall. Valerie quickly moved to Leblanc's side. In the center of the platform, she saw a device that looked like a bazooka. It had laser sights and a squeezable trigger; not very inviting at all.

"Zis, dear child," Leblanc explained as his fingers tapped around it, "is my invention. I call it, 'Ze Paralyzer.'"

"I don't like the sound of that," Valerie noted.

Leblanc continued. "Zis little gun allows me to paralyze aircraft with a zingle zhot. And when I zhoot its magnetic ray zrough zat porthole," Leblanc pointed to a thick window in the uneven ceiling above, "zen it can travel zrough ze water to take out ze vehicle's operating zystems. Zey never know what hits zem!" Leblanc squealed with delight.

"That's what you did to my SuperCopter," Valerie stated as she touched the barrel of the ray gun with her fingers. It was cold. "You tracked me, shot at me through the water with this ray, and paralyzed my 'Copter's electronics systems."

"Zen I waited for your aircraft to drop and zink. Immediately my taskbots recovered it and dismantled it. Brilliant, is it not?"

Valerie thanked God that the pirate really had no idea Alex's SuperCopter had been right behind hers. His shot must have knocked out both vessels by accident. And when the aircraft fused together, they appeared as one to his robots.

"Because you're hidden underwater, you can pick up the aircraft and be gone before help comes," Valerie said.

Leblanc nodded. He shrugged his shoulders, quite proud of himself. "I have found zat if I grab a zunken vessel and zen retreat to ze deep ocean, I can evade all detection. Zen I rise again, far away from my point of origin. Zat is why we are ztill zinking now. We will not ztart rising for zeveral hours."

"So where does the treasure come in?" Valerie asked.

Leblanc smiled. "Ze tour is not yet over."

The pirate turned, walked back to the ladder and headed down. As Valerie put her first foot on the ladder, her eyes drifted across the wide floor to the opposite side. A shudder crawled down her spine as she spotted a long piece of wood hinged backward into the ship. Valerie realized that if the roof were open and the wood were thrown the other way, it would be an instant walking plank. Somehow, she had a feeling she would see it again soon.

▲ ▲ ▲

The next—and last—stop on the tour was clear at the bottom of the ship, down four levels. When they came off the last ladder, Valerie recognized the hall. At the end was the door she'd entered when she and Alex had first split up. Leblanc didn't go through the door, but stopped short, choosing a door to the left instead. He slipped his access card into the lock and it popped open with a soft buzz.

Valerie's eyes had to adjust to the red lighting. From up on a platform, they observed the two taskbots dismantling arriving SuperCopter parts—many of which Valerie recognized from her aircraft maintenance courses at the Academy. She winced, hoping Leblanc didn't notice there were two air intake tri-folds sailing down the conveyor belt.

"So you capture aircraft and then take them apart," Valerie observed.

"Zis is my treasure," Leblanc said, holding his arms out wide. "Technology. Every piece is worth zomething zignificant."

Suddenly it hit Valerie. "So you're not building anything at all. You're selling the pieces for cash...harvesting aircraft."

Leblanc nodded his head. "Zis is part of my invention,

too. With a vessel's systems paralyzed and off-line, I can allow zem to zink. Zen, I bring zem aboard, put zem zrough a quick-drying process and zey are like new. My losses are minimal."

Valerie recalled the blast of air that had hit her and Alex when they'd first entered the coral ship. So that's what it was called…they were being "quick-dried." It really was ingenious…but still, it was wrong.

"How can you do this?" Valerie questioned. "It's just plain stealing!"

"I am a pirate!" Leblanc shouted, turning to her. "I am not a zaint like you."

Valerie wasn't about to argue with him. She decided to change the subject. "But to sell all this, you have to go on land, don't you?" she asked.

"I do not," Leblanc corrected. "I told you what I zink about zat. I am not going to risk *my* neck."

Valerie looked back at the conveyor belt, slowly sliding pieces down to the taskbots.

"Ophus," Valerie said. "You send Ophus to land to do your selling, don't you?"

Leblanc's voice took on an edge. He obviously wasn't pleased with her line of questioning. "He completes my business," the pirate said.

"And if he's caught, it's no skin off your nose."

"All zhips have a chain of command to protect ze captain!" Leblanc retorted.

"So basically you're using him," Valerie stated.

"His job is very important," Leblanc growled through clenched teeth. "He is my protection."

Valerie shook her head. "And who protects him?" she asked.

Leblanc didn't answer. "We are finished," he announced, walking out the door. Valerie followed. As the door shut, echoing through the hallway, Leblanc said, "I will zhow you to your room. You might as well get a good night's zleep. In less zan 12 hours we reach ze zurface."

Leblanc spun around on his heels and his eyes pierced Valerie's. "Zleep well, my dear. You will want to be wide awake for your last breath of fresh air."

6
Caught Red-Handed

From inside her room, Valerie peered out the miniature porthole window. The ocean was black as far as she could see. She could close her eyes and see the same thing. She had been confined against her will before, but this was somehow worse. She knew she was deep under the water, far from anyone's eyes or knowledge. A ray of sunlight would offer hope, but she could see none here. Leblanc didn't think this place was lonely, but Valerie couldn't understand that. To her, lonely was all it seemed to be. Well, lonely and beautiful…but the beauty diminished as time drew on.

"Even the depths can't separate me from Your love," Valerie prayed to the Lord, acknowledging Romans 8:38-39. She closed her eyes, forcing herself to put her faith in God. He would protect her, she was sure of it. That's what she had been taught all her life. She had experienced His protection before—quite dramatically at times. Growing up on Calypso Island, protection was an everyday experience. And even recently—during her visit to Jungle Island—she had been captured almost like this…and God had protected her from a burning fire.

Valerie wondered why time brought doubt. How is it that she could personally experience a miracle and then, later in life, when confronted with a similar situation, wonder if God would come through for her this time?

Valerie let out a long breath. No. She wouldn't wonder. God *would* come through. She wouldn't give in to the temptation of accepting a lie—of forgetting God's goodness to her. "Lord, You are good, and Your love endures forever," she said aloud. "Your faithfulness continues to all generations." Psalm 100:5. Her voice echoed in the room.

Valerie prayed in the spirit, letting the Holy Spirit speak through her lips. He reminded her to keep her thoughts on Him—to abide in Him, for with abiding comes protection and deliverance. "I will," she answered softly.

Valerie's thoughts drifted to Alex. She knew he was out there somewhere. She had tried to reach him via her ComWatch, but he didn't answer. She wondered if he was near. At least that would explain why he didn't answer. If he were near, he probably would have turned his ComWatch off so it wouldn't make any sudden noise. Ophus was right outside her door, and a sudden message on Alex's ComWatch would alert the big lug to his presence.

Valerie had tried to get through to Ophus when he was shoving her into her room. He wasn't a bad guy with twisted plans, like Leblanc. Ophus was just a simple man who was happy to help Leblanc out. He had no idea how his pirate "friend" was using him. Valerie had tried to share a few, brief words with him, but it seemed useless.

"Why do you work for that pirate?" she had asked as he strong-armed her into the room.

"The Captain is my friend," he'd said simply, lightening his grip.

Valerie's eyes had caught his as she'd asked, "Is he really?"

"The Captain gives me this job," Ophus had explained. He'd let go as Valerie entered the room.

"How much does he pay you?" Valerie had quizzed him. "Do you know that what he's doing is illegal?"

Ophus had just stared back at her, unable to answer the questions. Leblanc was using him and Ophus was following the pirate blindly.

As he closed the door to her room, Valerie had shouted, "He'll feed you to the sharks!"

Ophus had paused before shutting the door completely. He shook his head and said, "The Captain won't feed anyone to the sharks. The Captain is my friend." Then he'd closed the door tight. Valerie had heard him punch a keypad, and then the electronic lock clicked into place.

▲ ▲ ▲

Valerie sat up on her bed quickly when the door lock snapped open. Alex entered with a big, wide-toothed smile on his face. With a finger over his lips, he signaled Valerie to keep quiet. As quietly and quickly as she could, Valerie hopped off the bed. She threw her arms around Alex and gave him a big hug.

"We're on our way to the surface," Alex whispered. "It'll be a few more hours. Then we can launch the *Sentry* and get out of here—before either of them wakes up."

"You sure they're both asleep?" Valerie asked.

Alex nodded, angling his thumb over his shoulder. "I think so. The big guy is drooling outside your cabin. You know where we can get the pass card to the *Sentry?*"

Valerie nodded this time. "It should be on Leblanc's dresser."

"You guys are on a first name basis?" Alex asked.

"That's his last name. His full name is…um…oh yeah—'Jean-Luc Pierre Leblanc, ze zird,'" Valerie said, placing her hands on her hips. She lowered her voice. "'My father was a pirate, my grandfather was a pirate and my great-grandfather…well, he was a grocer, but never mind zat!'"

Alex stepped back. "You've spent some time with these guys, haven't you?"

"A little," Valerie admitted. "I'll fill you in on the way to Leblanc's room. How'd you get in here anyway?"

Alex smiled. "Touchpads are elementary," he said. Valerie smiled back. At times like this, she was thrilled that Alex was so good with electronics. She grabbed her friend's arm and they peeked out the doorway. Ophus was sitting in a metal chair, snoozing and snoring. The chair looked as if it was about to flatten under his weight.

"I feel sorry for him," Valerie whispered.

Alex's eyebrows bobbed up and down. "Well, it's his choice to be here."

Valerie shook her head. "I don't think he knows he has a choice," she said.

Then, slowly, the Superkids sneaked forward, out of the room and into the hallway.

Valerie pointed to the left. Alex followed her down the hall. Quietly, they made it around the corner without so much as a pin drop. Valerie stopped, turned, grabbed her friend's hand and bowed her head. She whispered, "Lord, I thank You that Your angels encamp 'round us and deliver us. I believe it because Psalm 34:7 says it. Guide us, Father. We thank You for Your everlasting protection."

"Amen," Alex agreed. Valerie let go of his hand and looked into his brown eyes.

"You must be starved," she said.

Alex smiled widely again. "Actually, I'm quite stuffed." He patted his stomach. "I found the kitchen."

"You raided his refrigerator?!" Valerie asked with a smile.

Alex nodded. "Yep."

"What'd you have?" Valerie asked, as if it mattered.

"Turkey legs," Alex replied. "The fridge was packed with them. This guy must not visit land but once in a blue moon."

"Well, he never does," Valerie said. "He sends Ophus."

Alex's forehead wrinkled. Valerie grabbed her friend's arm and began walking quietly again. As they made their way to Leblanc's room, she filled him in on all the details of her dinner with the pirate.

To Valerie's surprise, the open button to Leblanc's door shone green. The door was unlocked. Apparently the captain felt safe within his ship. She pressed the door open button, but held it down—a trick she had learned. Instead of flying open, the door slowly scooted aside. The room was dark, but inside, Valerie could hear the pirate's contented snore. Valerie let go of the button and the door sailed into its hideaway. Valerie placed her hand on the metal door jam. It was cold on her fingertips.

Quietly, she tiptoed into the room. At first, everything looked like nothing more than black blobs against black... but the longer she stood, the more her eyes adjusted and the more things took shape. She could make out the large dresser she had seen earlier, and Leblanc's king-sized bed with the pirate's figure lying on top. A small rectangle—the electronic *Treasure Island* book—was slowly heaving up and down on his chest, trapped beneath his clasped hands.

Valerie made her way over to the tall dresser, where she suspected the keycard would be. She ran her hand slowly along the top of the furniture, hoping to feel something. Her hand passed over a small box and some coins… but no card.

She looked over at Leblanc's nightstand, by his journal. The light hit the table just right and she could see it wasn't there.

"Psst! This it?"

Valerie's eyes shot up to Alex. He stood on the other side of Leblanc's bed.

“Alex!” Valerie whispered as quietly as she could. She was about to tell him he needed to get back to her side of the room in case he needed a quick getaway—but she didn’t. Instead, her eyes followed the line of his dark finger. He was pointing at the pirate’s curly, black beard. Lying outside the security of the blankets, from underneath a corner of his beard, Valerie saw it: a thin, leather strap. He was still wearing the plastic keycard. Valerie followed the leather string. It disappeared under the bobbing book he held on his chest. Valerie knew the card they needed was still attached to the string, under the book, under his folded hands.

Across the bed, Alex whispered, “What do we do?”

Valerie shrugged her shoulders. “Do we have a choice?”

Valerie looked down at Leblanc’s hands. Maybe, she thought, if she had a feather, she could tickle his foot like in the Larry and Jerry cartoons. Suddenly, with only a snort or two, Leblanc would let go and they’d be on their way home.

Carefully, Alex reached down and lifted the end of the book closest to Leblanc’s face with his fingertips. Just like in the cartoons, the pirate snorted and moved slightly, keeping the Superkids on edge. When he stilled, Valerie reached down and slowly pulled the card out by the leather string.

Alex squeezed his eyes shut.

"What?" Valerie whispered.

"His whiskers," Alex replied, "they're tickling my hand!" The pirate stirred again, mumbling something about Long John Silver.

"I've almost got it out!" Valerie announced as quietly as she could. With a soft yank, Valerie freed the card from beneath the book. She pulled it up into her palm as Alex set the book back down.

Alex looked at Valerie.

Valerie looked at Alex.

"How do we cut the string?" Alex wondered.

Valerie stood holding it in her hand. "I don't know." She looked around the room for something—anything—that could be used like a knife. Her eyes dropped to her ComWatch. "Alex—take off my ComWatch!" she whispered urgently. Alex had a questioning look on his face, but obeyed. With a snap, the watch popped off, and he handed it to her.

Swiftly, Valerie took the ComWatch's latch and pressed the leather strap against it. She was hoping it would be sharp enough to cut through the string with little effort.

Leblanc's feet moved.

Valerie and Alex froze.

Leblanc stilled.

Valerie began to saw like a tiny lumberjack. She passed the leather string over the latch again and again as fast as she could without waking the sleeping pirate. She wasn't sure if it was doing any good. If only she had a—

"Donga Donna Shoot!" shrieked Leblanc's parrot from the other side of the room.

Valerie screamed in surprise. Her ComWatch went flying.

Leblanc bolted up in bed.

Alex dropped to the floor.

Valerie turned on her heels to run, but slipped in her own tracks—Leblanc's strong hand was fastened around her wrist.

The parrot flew from wherever its perch was to the pirate's nightstand.

Valerie, twisting in midflight, tried to pull away from the pirate. It was no use. His dark, hollow eyes pierced her own. He began to laugh—first a chuckle, then a full-blown laugh-fest.

Valerie's eyebrows folded down. "My God will rescue me from your clutches," she promised, through clenched teeth.

Leblanc stopped laughing. "Enough with ze 'God talk.'" He lifted the plastic access card from his chest. "Zis—*zis* is what you came for?" He slapped it down against his chest. "It would not have mattered if you had gotten it. What are you going to do? Zteal away in ze *Zentry?* What? You do not zink I have it hooked to an alarm? Please," he scoffed. Then, at the top of his lungs, he shouted, "Ophus!"

Valerie heard the echo of Ophus' chair crashing down the hall, and then the big lug bounded to Leblanc's room. Valerie peered to the other side of the pirate's bed. Alex was down on the floor, out of sight. When Ophus arrived, he nearly stumbled back in surprise when he saw Valerie there. Leblanc threw her into his thick, hairy arms.

"Do not let her escape again!" he ordered. "Do your job!"

Ophus' grip on Valerie made her feel uncomfortable. "Ophus will hold the prisoner tight and not let her out," he said.

Leblanc stepped close, face to face with Ophus. "You had better," he scolded, "or I will feed you to ze zharks, too!"

Ophus stammered, but didn't say another word. He pulled Valerie into the hall and led her down to her prison.

A few turns later, he threw her in like a puppy pitched into the pound. "You won't get out this time," he said, fumbling with the door controls. The door shut quickly. Valerie heard the metal chair slam into the wall outside.

▲ ▲ ▲

"I am so tired," Valerie noted.

Alex nodded. "I'm exhausted, too. But the adrenaline keeps me going."

Both Superkids were kneeling beside the *Sentry,* Captain Leblanc's marine getaway vehicle. Alex was tinkering with the alarm system, attempting to disarm it. He had freed Valerie—for the second time—about two hours after the incident in Leblanc's quarters. The pirate still didn't know Alex was on board—an advantage the Superkids were using as often as possible.

According to Alex, after Ophus had locked Valerie in her room again, Alex had been able to retrieve the plastic access card. He'd had to wait until Leblanc fell asleep, but after he did, the Superkid had taken Valerie's ComWatch and sawed the card off the leather rope just as they'd planned. Then, upon returning to Valerie's quarters, he'd found Ophus asleep—again—which had made his second attempt at freeing Valerie as easy as the first.

Now both Superkids were free and, for the time being, Leblanc and Ophus were clueless. Time was getting shorter; they'd reach the surface in about two hours. Leblanc had the ship rising at minimal power, which increased the time before they reached the surface. Actually, they were slowly "drifting" up—an action which kept them hidden from radar, even those which measured subsurface tremors.

As Alex fiddled with the electronics, Valerie kept a lookout. The halls were silent.

Valerie rubbed the belly of the *Sentry.* It had a thick, fiberglass body, sealed together with long nuts and bolts. It was a rescue boat, really, designed for possible "break-down" if needed. One could take it apart and store it in an area a quarter the size of its mass. But Leblanc had no desire to take apart and store this two-person rescue vehicle. He used it for minimal transport between the land and sea. Valerie imagined that he attached some sort of sea trailer for larger loads.

Currently, the *Sentry* was locked down to the main ship with a pair of squared, metal arms—Leblanc's security measure. If the Superkids could unlock the arms, they could open the doors and launch the boat at just the right time.

"I think I'm ready," Alex said.

Valerie turned to her friend. She placed a hand on his arm. "Thank you, Alex," she said. "I didn't mean to step out so far and get us into all this."

"Hey," Alex replied, "sometimes you have to step out beyond your comfort zone and let your faith take over."

"Well, I stepped way out on this one. I'm sorry."

Alex shook his head. "There's nothing to be sorry about. We've found what we came to find."

Valerie knew he was right, but it still slightly pained her to think of everything she had put them both through. Things could have turned out differently. She closed her eyes and thanked God again for His protection. Things hadn't turned out exactly the way she had hoped they would, but it all worked out in the end. Part of her was glad the whole adventure was about to be over. She was tired, and she wasn't sure her faith would carry her through if things got much worse.

Valerie froze at the thought. Did that thought really just run through her mind? Of course her faith would carry her through…wouldn't it? *Lord, I make my thoughts come into obedience with Your Word, according to 2 Corinthians 10:5. You will not forsake Your faithful ones. They will be protected forever,* Valerie prayed Psalm 37:28 silently. Well, at least for now, she wouldn't have to test her faith…

"Here we go," Alex said. He pulled Valerie's Com-Watch out of his pocket. Valerie smiled.

"You found it," she stated.

"It's been rather handy," he returned. Then he used the latch to slice through a yellow wire. "This should disarm it," he explained.

"You know, we could have stopped in the kitchen to get a knife," Valerie pointed out.

Alex smirked. "Why take the easy road?"

Snap! The wire cut.

Valerie dropped Leblanc's security card into the launch slot. The metal arms surrounding the boat slowly opened. Then silence.

It worked.

It worked! In two hours—before Leblanc or Ophus even awakened, they'd open the launch door and speed away!

WHOOP! WHOOP! WHOOP! WHOOP!

"What's that?!" Valerie cried at the sound of the siren. Her hands started shaking.

Alex gulped. "It's the alarm."

7
"Donga Donna Shoot!"

Valerie grabbed her ComWatch from Alex. "You sure we can't launch the Sentry now?!"

"Sure we can," Alex said, "but we'll be launching straight into the ocean. It'll sink before it swims—blowing our only opportunity to get off this ship!"

"HEY!" the pirate's voice resounded through the hall, startling Valerie and Alex. Leblanc and Ophus stood at the far end of the walkway, Leblanc in a deep purple robe. He slapped a panel on the wall, shutting down the piercing alarm.

"Get zem!" he commanded Ophus, pointing a finger at the Superkids. Upon receiving his order, the big guy bounded down the hall.

"Let's get out of here!" Valerie cried, leaping forward. She and Alex took off in the opposite direction from their captors.

"The pass card!" Alex shouted as they ran. "It's still in the launch slot!"

"Forget it!" Valerie shouted back, as if they really had a choice.

Boom-boom-boom-boom! The Superkids ran down the hall, their foot-stomps echoing off the metal floor.

"Where did zat other kid come from?!" Leblanc screamed, his pride hurt. He launched after them, too.

"This way!" Valerie cried, grabbing Alex's arm. They turned down one corridor after another, hearing Ophus' thundering footsteps behind them.

Valerie looked left and then right at the next intersection. The hallways looked identical.

"I'm lost," she said quickly. "We could be going in circles."

"There!" Alex shouted, pointing to the left. Valerie saw it too. A ladder heading down.

"Let's go! Let's go!" Valerie pushed, already running.

The Superkids dropped down the ladder. They halted.

Valerie caught her breath. "You think we lost them?" she asked, bent with her hands on her knees. Alex nodded. She wiped the perspiration from her forehead.

Suddenly the ladder shook. Valerie and Alex looked up.

"You stop!" Ophus shouted from above. He threw himself onto the ladder.

"He's not going to give up, is he?" Alex asked.

Valerie shook her head. "Neither are we." She looked down the hall. All the doors were closed and the door opening buttons were red.

"We have to find another ladder and go as deep as we can," Valerie said. "You said you found a junkyard down there. Maybe we can hide in it."

Alex nodded and the two Superkids were off. They shot down the hall, following its twists and turns. Behind them, they heard Ophus land on the same level and start running.

Periodically Valerie and Alex would slap a door open button as they ran, hoping one would miraculously pop open. None did.

Another ladder, and they dropped another level. Valerie made the executive decision to go right at the bottom. It was a good decision that landed them at the last ladder, heading directly to the bottom level.

With a thump, they leapt to the ground and took off flying. Ophus was still close behind. His big feet, were already in sight, coming down the last ladder. The Superkids raced down the hall to the same big, steel door Valerie had used to get into the ship's halls in the first place.

"Let it still be unlocked," she said as a prayer between breaths.

SLAP! Valerie smashed the door open button and the door slid open. The Superkids ran inside and quickly closed the door behind them.

"Now where?" Alex asked, peering into the empty room where their SuperCopters had once stood. Two taskbots were shut down on the far side of the room, recharging.

Valerie ran down the short stairs, two at a time. "Onto the conveyor belt," she said. They hopped on top of it and quickly crawled into the black hole where Valerie had earlier seen the SuperCopter parts and Alex disappear.

Boom! Ophus crashed into the room. Valerie held her breath as they rode the conveyor belt, everything growing dark. The conveyor belt passage was long and black. Alex touched her on the shoulder. "Let me go in first," he whispered, moving in front of her, "I know the room a little better. I think I know just where to hide."

Ahead, Valerie saw the end approaching. She began to make out Alex's frame. She looked back to see if Ophus was coming, but didn't see him. Still, she kept herself ready for anything.

"Aaahhhh!"

Valerie spun around when Alex shouted. At the end of the passageway, Alex was grabbed by two meaty hands—Ophus!

Valerie screamed and grabbed onto Alex. Together, the Superkids were dragged off the conveyor belt. Alex pushed and Valerie kicked, but Ophus was unmovable. The giant of a man grunted and kicked back at Valerie, sending her flying. She smashed into a pile of metal scraps, barely missing a bulky taskbot. Valerie got up and grabbed a piece of metal.

"Run, Valerie!" Alex shouted.

"I'm not leaving without you!" Valerie cried, tightening her grip on the metal. She didn't want to use it, but...

SLAM! The door to the inventory room opened and the pirate stepped through. His dark beard seemed to melt into his dark purple robe. "And what do you plan to do with zat?" he asked Valerie. He slowly walked down a series of metal steps, taking his place beside Ophus. His parrot flew into the room, its wings crackling the air. It landed on its master's shoulder and stared at Valerie with beady eyes.

"Donga donna shoot!" it squawked.

"Run, Valerie!" Alex shouted again. "You can make it!"

Valerie looked at the door. She *might* be able to make it, *if* Leblanc wasn't able to grab her first. She looked at the metal scrap in her hand. Maybe if she slapped his arm with it on her way out he'd fumble and she'd get a head start. Maybe...but not likely.

"God's hand will sustain me; surely His arm will

strengthen me…No wicked man will oppress me," Valerie quoted Psalm 89:21-22 just loud enough for her own ears to hear.

She didn't want to leave Alex, but if she didn't, they'd both be caught. If only there was another way of escape. Suddenly Valerie remembered the verse Alex had spoken to her earlier: Daniel 3:17—"Our God whom we serve is able to deliver us." Her eyes scanned the room. There had to be a way out of this…

There! Valerie saw it! One of the taskbots at the far side of the room opened a panel next to a dark, oceanic window. The panel was small, but just big enough to crawl inside. The taskbot dumped a bucket into it. A garbage chute, perhaps? Valerie didn't care. It had to lead somewhere. Maybe to a whole series of chutes that could take her anywhere in the ship. It was worth a shot. She looked at Leblanc. Now for something he didn't expect…

Valerie stood her ground until the taskbot moved close enough…then…*boom!* Valerie slammed into the robot, shoulder first, with full force. The taskbot shifted paths and headed straight at Leblanc. It bought her the time she needed. Valerie sprinted across the room. She slapped the panel's open button and, with a wave, she jumped inside. Just as she triumphantly dove in, she heard Leblanc laugh and the parrot squawk again, "Donga donna shoot!" Only this time, for some reason, the parrot's words made sense.

Leblanc's feathered friend was telling her something. Something she didn't want to hear.

He was screaming a warning that would ring in her ears again and again.

He was telling her, "Don't go down the chute!"

▲ ▲ ▲

Like a roller coaster ride, Valerie slid down a gooey incline. It wasn't that steep, but she had dived in with such force, she had a hard time stopping. She went down…down…down.

Ka-thump!

Valerie landed in the center of a wide cylinder. She looked up and saw that the cylinder continued above her. Small red lights that served no apparent purpose lined the cylinder. She was right about the trash system chutes converging together…but she was wrong about *where* they converged. This was where they ended—and the only chute she could reach was the one she had just slid down. Valerie let out a long breath. Going back up and facing Leblanc again was not her idea of a good time.

Valerie looked at her feet. She was standing in a pile of

scraps the taskbot had just tossed down. She tried to lift a foot and heard her shoe crackle as she pulled it off the sticky floor. She tried not to think of how disgusting it really was.

The air was thinner here—she could feel herself breathing heavier, trying to make up the difference. A dense petroleum smell burned her eyes, nose and lungs. Valerie yelped in surprise when some scraps crashed down on her from above. She tried to dodge the blows, but the cylinder was too small. Something landed on her shoulder and she shook it off. When it fell to her feet, it caught her eye—it was a half-eaten turkey leg. She picked it up and looked at it. Petroleum goo dripped off the remaining meat and bone.

"Gross! Gross! Gross!" Valerie shouted, tears coming to her eyes.

Shoom! The tube above her head sealed. She was suddenly confined to a space not much bigger than herself. Valerie took a deep breath in surprise.

Foom! The ground beneath her popped open and salty ocean water flooded in immediately. Valerie instinctively held her breath. The force of the water shot her and the garbage out into the ocean water. Valerie flipped around in the current, trying to gain her perspective. She knew she didn't have much breath—she had to think fast. Through Academy training courses she had learned to hold her breath for a long time...but not *that* long.

She swam out a short distance before she looked back. Before her, Valerie saw the looming coral ship. The interior lights were on and she could see inside. There—from the inventory room—she saw Alex, Leblanc, Ophus and the parrot staring back at her.

She *had* to get back inside. The ocean was bare—no underwater stations or rescue ships as far as she could see.

Suddenly a small shadow passed over a section of the coral ship. It was something swimming...something Valerie recognized too easily. A shark.

Valerie wanted to panic, wanted to scream, but she knew she couldn't. Her heart was beating fast. The shark had seen her. It was moving toward her. She had to act quickly. There was nowhere to run or hide.

She looked at her hand. It still clutched the turkey leg.

The God Whom you serve is able to deliver you, Valerie's spirit reminded her.

Valerie was desperate. She latched onto the promise and felt her faith arise. *Yes! God is able to deliver me!* Valerie stared at the approaching shark—and saw the light. The dim, red light. It was coming from the open hatch she had just exited. It hadn't closed yet.

The shark approached.

Valerie's lungs burned.

Her eyes focused on the hatch.

A thousand thoughts ran through her mind. What if she didn't make it? What if the shark got to her first? What if she ran out of breath? Why did she force herself and Alex onto this crazy pirate's ship in the first place?

Valerie stopped her thoughts.

She focused on one thing.

Jesus. Jesus! He was all that mattered. He was going to help her. *He was able.*

The hungry shark was nearly upon her. Valerie let go of the turkey leg with a thrust of her hand. The shark's eyes followed the fresh meat and its body followed. The big fish caught the bone in its jaws and instantly chomped it to bits.

Valerie didn't waste the opportunity. She swam forward with full force and kicked herself into the garbage chute exit. The very moment she got inside, the door shut beneath her, her mouth opened for air as the water quickly dispensed.

Valerie coughed and wheezed, sucking in air as fast as she could. Her chest burned like fire, as did her nose and throat. Feeling weak, Valerie crawled back up the gooey slide. For some reason, she didn't care that Leblanc was on the other side. With each move forward she felt her faith solidifying, her boldness hardening, her strength returning.

Still coughing, Valerie reached the top of the chute. With both fists, she pounded open the chute panel, sending it flying into the room. She exited and stood up straight, staring at the pirate through her dark, wet hair.

Leblanc, with a wide smile on his face, applauded. "What entertainment!" he shouted.

"Donga donna shoot!" his bird warned.

"No kidding," Valerie responded. The air was cleaner in the room and she began to feel better immediately. A puddle of ocean water was forming at her feet.

Valerie clasped her fists together. The goo on her hands made them sticky. She opened her fists, held her palms up in front of her and walked toward Leblanc. At once, the pirate pulled out a small knife and stopped her in her tracks.

"Do not touch me with zat ztuff," he ordered. Valerie reluctantly complied. "My parrot almost died last year when he flew into ze garbage zhute out of curiosity. Fortunately, his feet got ztuck to ze zide and

I was able to retrieve him."

"Donga donna shoot!" the bird yelped again.

"It made a lasting impression," the pirate added.

Valerie just stared at the pirate. He was unbelievable. She held up her hands in front of him. "This is why there's no life out there, isn't it?" she demanded. "You take this route all the time…and you deposit your toxic waste into the ocean, killing all the surrounding life. That also explains why the sharks are hungry enough to attack people!"

"Zpare me ze lecture," Leblanc said with a wave of his small, silver knife. "I did not get where I am following all ze rules."

"Keep breaking them and you won't get much further."

"I will escort you to your room."

"No thanks, I know where it is."

"Zuch arrogance. Where does it come from?"

"My assurance comes from knowing my God is going to rescue us," Valerie said. "He'll do it—just like He rescued me just now."

"Zat?" Leblanc asked, pointing his knife to the window. "Zat was luck! We zhall zee what happens in a few hours when we reach ze zurface."

"Where's Alex?" she demanded.

Leblanc nodded at the door with his head. "Ophus has

taken him to ze brig."

Valerie turned. It wasn't worth giving him her time. She marched toward the stairs, the pirate close behind.

"I will enjoy having two plank walkings," he muttered.

Valerie spun around. "What? No! Let me walk—but not Alex. This isn't his fault."

"Why zhould he not walk as well?" the pirate asked.

"Because he's…well, he's a technical whiz," she said, trying to appeal to the pirate's pride. "He could be valuable to you. Very valuable."

"I have run zis zhip for years without extra help. But…hmm…it is worth consideration anyway." Then he added, "What about you? Are you valuable in any way?"

Valerie was ready to blurt out again that God would protect her, but her eyes dropped to her clothes. They were wet and gooey and suddenly she didn't feel like much of a witness. How could Leblanc see what had just happened and call it "luck"?! It was God's protection! Wasn't it?! God had protected her because she was His child, hadn't He? Because *He* saw her as valuable, right?

Valerie couldn't find the words to answer him.

8
Bruised and Worn

Valerie lay on the bed in her holding room. Thank God for little favors; the room had an adjoining bathroom where she could wash up. Full of thankfulness, she got all the goop out of her hair and off her hands. There was even a hair dryer in there—she used it to dry her hair and her clothes after washing them.

She walked back into the bedroom, feeling refreshed, and walked over to the small porthole window. She looked outside at the ocean blackness. A little light was playing on the current—revealing waves of dark blue here and there. It was a welcome indication that they were near the surface. After being trapped in the dungeon of the coral ship, the hint of real sunlight was refreshing. Valerie let out a long, thoughtful breath. It had been less than 24 hours, but it seemed like it had been an eternity. She thought it always seemed like an eternity when she was forced to wait for the inevitable.

Quietly she prayed in the spirit, asking the Lord to give her wisdom about what to do, and when. It bothered her that she had questions. It bothered her that she felt so strongly about the Lord's protection and then, with just a few words, Leblanc had stolen her thunder.

"It was luck," he had said. She'd heard that before. *"Beginner's luck." "Good luck." "Aren't you lucky."* Valerie didn't believe it. She had been shot into the ocean without warning, hunted down by a man-eating shark—and she just *happened* to have a half-eaten turkey leg still clutched in her hand? That was just too much to be coincidence. The Lord had orchestrated things. He knew what was going to happen long before she did. She believed His promises and He protected her. After all, He had done it before—many times!

Valerie remembered the last time she had been stuck in a room like this, waiting for the inevitable. It was in the Manwan village on Jungle Island. They had accused Valerie of trespassing and were ready to pronounce her death. But the Lord had protected her—more than once. Valerie's faith stirred as she recalled how the Lord had come through. So why did what Leblanc had said bother her? How could he have stolen her thunder?

Valerie thought of him standing there in his royal-looking, purple robe, secure in his pirate plans, proud that his evil ways were going so well for him. That's why it bothered her. Because *Leblanc* didn't see it. He stood there, blinded to God's workings because he thought he had the whole world under *his* control.

If the Lord suddenly showed up helping someone, that would mean Captain Jean-Luc Pierre Leblanc wasn't in absolute control. That would mean there is an absolute God with absolute standards—rules Leblanc was breaking. Rules Leblanc would be *responsible* for breaking. Suddenly pirating couldn't be justified as noble…and Leblanc wouldn't be able to handle that. But that's why it bothered Valerie: The pirate was blinded. He couldn't look at creation and see God. He destroyed creation. He couldn't look at the light of the Lord in God's people. He had disconnected from people. He had hardened his heart long ago…and Valerie saw no way to break through to him. There seemed to be no miracle he wouldn't explain away.

Valerie lifted her wrist and tapped her ComWatch. It buzzed and bleeped. It was in pretty bad shape after cruising the depths of the ocean with her. She and Alex had toasted three ComWatches in less than 24 hours. *That has to be a record,* she thought.

To her surprise, Alex's face actually appeared on her watch, even though it was three shades of purple.

"Hey," she said, "I'm glad I got you. I tried earlier, but you didn't answer."

"Leblanc was here quizzing me about my technical knowledge," Alex responded. "I turned the ComWatch off so he wouldn't realize we could communicate." Alex smiled slightly. "What did you say to him, anyway? He says he wants to keep me around long enough to drain my 'technological wisdom.'"

"Ah," Valerie punctuated, not answering the question. "Where are you?"

"Some jail cell on Level 3," Alex answered. "It's actually not that bad. It's not as nice as *your* quarters, but it's livable."

Valerie bit her bottom lip. "Look, I know you're probably tired of hearing it, but I'm really sorry I got you into this. I didn't mean to lead you wrong."

"You didn't, Val," Alex said. "God will protect us."

Valerie nodded. "I know He will. Part of me just wants to tell Him exactly how to do it, though."

Alex smiled warmly.

"I just don't want to be in a situation where I don't know if I'm walking in faith or not. I want to *know,* you know?"

"Just stand on His promises to you," Alex offered, "and the situations will take care of themselves."

Valerie just looked at Alex's purple face for a long

moment, then she said, "Well, let's keep praying."

"Alex out."

▲ ▲ ▲

The sun hurt Valerie's eyes. She looked away from it and down at her bare feet. They stood at the edge of a long, wooden plank, hanging over rolling waves. Shark fins circled beneath her.

"Run, Valerie!" Alex shouted. Valerie looked and saw him held tightly by Ophus. Leblanc was standing at the other end of the plank, between them, with his silver knife catching the sunlight, threatening Valerie's return.

"Run, Valerie!"

Snap! Valerie nearly lost her balance when the shark popped out of the water and bit the air. It was just waiting for her to jump in, its dingy teeth hungry for a good meal.

The struggle ran through her mind—would God rescue her? Protect her? What if she stepped out, but didn't *really* believe? What if she wasn't ready?

No—she had to be ready. She *had* to be ready. She had to make a choice.

"Run, Valerie!" Alex shouted again, his voice ringing in her ears. Leblanc tossed his knife at the plank. It stuck in the wood blade-first. He laughed and clapped.

"What entertainment!" he shouted.

"I'm sorry," Valerie whispered to Alex.

Leblanc's parrot launched off the pirate's shoulder and flew around Valerie's head. "Donga inna wata!" it squawked again and again.

Valerie felt the panic rise in her heart. She had to do something, *something!*

She closed her eyes and took a step forward, off the plank. What else was she to do?

Thump!

Valerie opened her eyes. She had landed *on top* of the water. Her feet were rolling up and down on the waves! She was walking on water!

She'd done it! She'd walked out in faith—it was no mistake! God had protected her!

Snap! Valerie let out a scream as one of the sharks popped out of the water and launched at her feet. She jumped sideways and landed, but her feet went straight down into the raging sea. Her whole body followed and suddenly she found herself gasping for air.

Where did God go? Where was His protection now?! Valerie screamed again, taking in half a mouthful of salt water. She kicked and swam as fast as she could. Maybe she could get away from the sharks if she swam hard enough. Maybe…

▲ ▲ ▲

A rap on the steel door awoke Valerie with a start. Her heart was racing and it took her a few minutes to shake the bad dream from her head. She whispered a quiet "Thank You" to the Lord, relieved it wasn't real. Then she froze when she saw the bright light coming through the port-hole. They had reached the surface. No it wasn't real…but it would be any minute...

Valerie couldn't recall when she'd fallen asleep. She knew she had been praying for a long time, but her under-water adventure had worn her. Her exhausted body had claimed its rest. Slowly she arose, shaking the sleepiness from her head.

She walked to the door, wondering what would happen if she didn't answer. Could she stay in the room forever and avoid walking the plank?

The knock came again.

Valerie approached the door. "Who is it?" she asked, not sure what else to say.

"It's Ophus," the big, burly guy outside her door said.

"What do you want?" Valerie asked, as if he might

have an answer that would surprise her.

"Ophus wants to say 'hi,'" he said.

Valerie blinked. The answer did surprise her. "Okay," she said. "Hi."

A long pause followed. Then with a click, the lock released and the door slid open. "Captain fed you to the sharks," Ophus said, staring at the ground.

Valerie stared at Ophus' bald head. Then, placing her fingertips under his chin, Valerie lifted his eyes to hers. He looked sad—no, *scared*—Valerie could see it. The man he trusted with his life…the pirate he called his friend…had crossed a boundary Ophus didn't want crossed. And it scared him.

"Captain isn't good," he added.

Valerie touched the man's arm. "It's important you do the right thing, Ophus. Don't worry about me. God will take care of me."

"Ophus needs protection," the big lug said in a pitiful voice. Valerie's heart sank.

"I can't help you right now," Valerie said. "But I know Someone Who can."

Ophus looked into Valerie's eyes with wonderment. For the first time, Valerie noticed that his bloodshot eyes were blue.

"*God* can help you," Valerie explained. "Listen to me, Ophus. God sent Jesus, His Son, to earth, to pay for your wrongs so you wouldn't have to pay for them yourself. That payment was death. But Jesus rose again so you could have life."

Ophus' forehead wrinkled as he thought about what she was saying.

"God has already protected you from hell and death," Valerie said. "He's paid the price. It's nothing for Him to protect you from anything else. You just have to put your full trust—your full life—in His hands."

Ophus turned and looked down the hall. "You believe that?" he asked Valerie, turning to her again, looking at a large bruise above her right elbow. Valerie covered it up with her hand.

"I do," she said.

Ophus nodded and looked down the hall again. "Captain's coming," he announced. He quickly closed the door.

Valerie leaned back against the steel and felt it press against her back. Why did she feel like not only was her life on the line, but like she was also trying to pass some sort of test?

She waited as she heard muffled voices outside.

Moments later, the door opened and Ophus grabbed her arm, his grip not as tight as usual.

"Good morning," Leblanc greeted her. He was dressed in his deep purple shirt, black and gold hat and black velvet pants again. His beard and earrings were perfectly in place. His parrot sat on his shoulder. "It is your zpecial day."

Valerie narrowed her eyes. "God will protect me," she said, not as strongly as she would have liked.

"Zis I have got to zee," the pirate mocked. Then he added, "I was going to feed you breakfast, but zen I zought, *why?*" His laughter echoed in the halls.

The pirate turned to Ophus. "Go get ze boy." Ophus obeyed.

"Alex?" Valerie cried. "What are you going to do to Alex?"

The pirate turned and started walking. Valerie followed.

"Nothing, for now," Leblanc responded. "I just did not want him to miss zaying goodbye to you. It makes for a more dramatic zene."

Wonderful, Valerie thought, *a pirate with a flair for drama.*

Leblanc clapped his hands. "I can hardly wait."

9

Walking the Plank

The hatch to the platform was open when they arrived. Valerie squinted at the bright, early morning sunlight. It immediately played warmly on her skin, giving her goose bumps. After being stuck inside the coral ship for so long, it felt *wonderful.* The sweet smell of sea air filled her nostrils and actually brought a weak smile to her lips. Leblanc offered his hand to Valerie as she came to the top of the ladder; she didn't take it.

The lulling rush of ocean waves hit Valerie's ears and reminded her of Calypso Island, where she'd grown up. *It wouldn't be bad to be there now,* she thought. A cool, steady breeze brushed her face, reminding her that whether she liked it or not, she was in the middle of nowhere, in the middle of the ocean.

The platform looked similar to when she'd last seen it, but the domed covering was folded back into the base of the coral ship. To her far left was the Paralyzer ray, sitting dormant, yet ominous. To her far right were Ophus and Alex. The big guy had his thick hands on Alex's shoulders. Valerie knew her friend wasn't going anywhere. And in front of Valerie was the plank she had seen earlier. It was flipped now, stretching out into the ocean, hovering over it, vibrating with the waves.

Valerie looked up. A few long, white cloud wisps looked like scratches across the blue sky.

"Well, let us get zis zhow on ze road," Leblanc prodded. He grinned at a sudden thought, "Or zhould I zay, on ze plank?" He put his hand behind Valerie's head and began walking forward. The force of his push made Valerie stumble alongside him, involuntarily. As they drew closer, Valerie was able to see over the side of the ship. In the distance, small, gray fins appeared periodically. Sharks were near, hoping for food from the coral ship.

"I took ze liberty to zrow in a few appetizers," Leblanc explained. "Ze zharks are looking forward to zeir main course."

Valerie felt the heat rising in her body.

No. She refused to let fear take over.

Valerie glanced back at Alex. He stood there, looking at her, not saying a word. Valerie had told Ophus to do his job, and he was. Alex wasn't going to get away. Part of Valerie wondered if she should have told Ophus something different. Maybe she could have set up some kind of elaborate plan that would set her free at the last minute. But it was too late for that now. If only she had known sooner that Ophus didn't care for being in Leblanc's service. And Alex…he had no idea that Ophus had questions. So much for elaborate plans.

Strangely enough, even though her life was on the line, Valerie found her thoughts circling around other things. She wondered what would happen to Ophus and Alex. And what about Leblanc? How many more aircraft would he sink and rip apart for his own gain? Would there be any other pilots he would make walk his wooden plank? Valerie looked at the sky again. If only she had more time.

Leblanc was standing at the front of the plank, smiling. "Zo," he said, "any last requests?"

Valerie shook her head. "My God will protect me," she said to him. "Psalm 91 says if you make the Most High your dwelling, then no harm will befall you and no disaster will come. That's what I believe. God's Word is true. He *will* protect me."

Leblanc stood aside. He scanned Valerie up and down. Valerie knew he was looking at her bruises and scratches from the past 24 hours. He was wondering how she could be so foolish as to believe God would protect her. If He would, then where was He when she'd gotten bruised and scratched from head to toe?

No. Valerie pushed aside the doubting thoughts again. She wouldn't think about all that. She knew she didn't have all the answers, but she had *The Answer.* Jesus would save her. He would protect her. She planted her feet firmly on the ship's hull.

"Time for ze festivities," Leblanc said. Then after a pause, he ordered, "Walk ze plank."

"No," Valerie said, standing her ground.

The pirate squinted his eyes, staring down at Valerie with those dark eyebrows hovering over his face.

"Walk ze plank!" he shouted, his voice carrying in the wind.

Valerie didn't move. The parrot squawked.

Leblanc's eyes shot over to his first mate. "Ophus!" he shouted. "Move her onto ze plank!"

Ophus started to move, but hesitated. He looked into Valerie's eyes and then back to Leblanc's.

"Move her onto ze plank!" Leblanc ordered again.

"You are not my Lord," Ophus said to his captain.

Leblanc's head tilted and his cheeks flushed. "I am your lord and captain!" he shouted, spitting.

Ophus let go of Alex. "Not anymore," he said plainly.

Valerie smiled. Alex was visibly surprised. Leblanc was furious.

The pirate shouted in frustration. And, just as Alex started to move forward, Leblanc whipped out his small, silver knife. "Not another ztep," he said, pressing the flat side of the blade into Valerie's side.

Valerie looked at the sky and then closed her eyes. The inevitable was waiting.

"Go," the pirate commanded Valerie. He pressed the blade harder against her side. Against her will, Valerie stepped aside and her feet hit the plank. Her stomach turned. Out of the corner of her eye, she could see a shark fin.

Valerie scanned the bridge as quickly as she could. Ophus, Alex, Leblanc—there was no apparent way of escape.

The God Whom we serve is able to deliver us, Alex had reminded her. But where was His deliverance? Valerie turned around and faced the plank. The sharks circled nearby. Leblanc slid in behind her and she was forced to move forward again.

If I just had more time! Lord, where is Your protec—NO! Valerie refused to let her faith drift. She took three steps forward. She was at the end of the plank.

"Jesus! Jesus! Jesus!" her mouth said as her mind and spirit put their trust in Him.

SLAM!

Leblanc kicked the wooden plank and it shifted fast, throwing Valerie off balance. Valerie's arms flew up and her knees buckled. She almost screamed, but just cried, "Jesus! Jesus!" again. The plank cracked aside and Valerie crashed into the water, back first. Bubbles and liquid encompassed her, swallowing her like a gigantic bowl of gelatin.

She twisted and turned, searching for the surface. She had barely had a chance to get any air. Her lungs were already hurting. But Valerie kept her focus—her thoughts and prayers—steadied on one thing: *Jesus! Jesus!*

Valerie's head cracked through the water's surface, and her mouth opened, gasping for air. A big gulp of it filled her lungs, along with a spattering of salt water. Valerie shook the hair out of her face as she treaded in the water. Above, Leblanc laughed as he watched her. Alex and Ophus were standing beside him, looking out at Valerie, too far away to reach.

Valerie reached forward to take a swimming stroke toward the coral ship when her hand hit a mass of gray flesh. She retracted her arm when she saw the shark. It came right at her, a hungry look in its eye.

THUMP! The shark pounded into Valerie's ribs, hitting

her hard, but bouncing back. Another shark hit her from the side, thumping into her arm.

Jesus! Jesus!

THUMP! THUMP! THUMP! From the back, side and front, the sharks hit her, each one taking its turn and then circling and attacking from another angle.

THUMP! THUMP! THUMP!

Up on the coral ship, Leblanc's chin dropped. "Why do zey not open zeir mouths and eat her?!" he shouted at the top of his lungs.

Ophus stared in wonderment. "God is protecting Valerie," he said simply.

"I cannot believe zis!" Leblanc shouted, throwing his knife across the ship in a fit of rage. It slapped to the ground and rolled.

Alex laughed aloud. "Valerie—they're gumming you!" he shouted.

Valerie's eyes were wide as she watched the sharks come at her, lightly hit her body and bounce back. They wouldn't open their mouths—they *couldn't* open their mouths!

At once, Valerie found herself out of breath again. But this time it wasn't from being ejected from a SuperCopter. It wasn't from being too deep underwater without air. It wasn't from running too hard or from being too scared. Valerie's breath was suddenly taken away by the awesomeness of her God. He loved her. He was protecting her. And He was faithful to His Word, faithful to His promises. This time, believing Him *was* her deliverance from disaster. *He was able!*

Enveloped in God's perfect love, Valerie swam to the coral ship, completely free from fear. The pirate wasn't able to steal Valerie's life. She was one craft he wasn't going to sink.

When Valerie reached the edge, Ophus bent down and lifted her up with one arm. Just as he set her down on the deck, Leblanc came rushing furiously forward at Ophus. Just before the pirate crashed into him, Ophus let go of Valerie and stood up straight. Leblanc smashed into Ophus and pushed as hard as he could. Ophus stood still.

"Captain trying to feed Ophus to the sharks?" he asked with his deep voice. Leblanc tried pushing three more times, but couldn't budge the big guy.

"Hey, try picking on someone your own size!" Alex said, laughing. Leblanc stopped pushing.

"It wouldn't matter if you *were* strong enough to push him in," Valerie said to the pirate. "He serves a new Lord now—a Lord Who protects His children who put their faith in Him."

Then Valerie added, "It's over Captain Jean-Luc Pierre Leblanc."

Leblanc's eyes moved from Valerie to Ophus to Alex.

"It is not over!" Leblanc challenged.

"This isn't going to end like one of your pirate novels," Valerie said. "It's going to end for you just like it did for all those other pirates you told me about. Sin has its payment. Too bad you're without protection."

Leblanc huffed and spun around, walking toward the ladder. "I am taking us back down!"

Bzzzz—pop!

The pirate froze at the sound and fixed his eyes on Valerie. "What was zat?"

Valerie tapped on her ComWatch. "It's my communications watch," she said. "Someone's trying to reach me."

Suddenly Alex's ComWatch flashed on. Alex looked down and smiled. "It's *our* captain," he announced.

"Hello, Alex," Commander Kellie's face said from his ComWatch. "It's good to see you. We'll be there shortly. Kellie out."

"What?!" Leblanc cried.

Alex pulled a small, silver cylinder out of his pocket.

"The moment I got up here, I started transmitting our coordinates with my homing beacon."

The pirate snatched the device out of Alex's hand and smashed it on the deck.

"Our ComWatches are short range," Valerie added. "In a matter of minutes a whole fleet of SuperCopters will be on their way to help us…and apprehend you."

"Nooooo!!!" Leblanc screamed as he peered into the sky. Tearing through the distant streaks of white clouds were 10 SuperCopters with one destination: Captain Leblanc's coral ship.

The pirate stomped on the beacon for emphasis, then glanced to his right. He smiled. "Let zem come," he said. "Let zem come."

10

Val's Best Shot

Like a flock of birds, the SuperCopters flew over the ocean, drawing closer to the coral ship by the moment. The sight of the rescue party put huge smiles on Valerie and Alex's faces. Here came the cavalry. Valerie looked forward to throwing her arms around her commander and close friend. It would be so good to see her. For some reason, Valerie didn't care about hearing whether she'd done a good job or not. She just wanted to get out of the world of pirates with planks to be walked.

The SuperCopters drew nearer and nearer. Soon it would all be over.

Sha-POWWWWWWWWWWW!!!!! Valerie screamed as the deafening noise broke the air. She and Alex hit the deck and covered their ears.

"What was that?!" Valerie cried to Alex.

"I don't know!" Alex shouted back. Valerie's eyes darted over to Leblanc, answering her own question. Across the deck, Leblanc was standing at the Paralyzer ray, his hands tightly around the control panel. He was charging it again. Valerie looked out at the approaching

SuperCopters and saw one diving into the ocean.

Sploosh! The aircraft collided with the waves. The pilot had already ejected and looked like a plastic army figure drifting down in a parachute.

Valerie got to her knees. She had to stop Leblanc.

Sha-POWWWWWWWWWWW!!!!! Valerie screamed again. Leblanc's parrot was squawking fiercely, flying around haphazardly.

Zap! The ray hit another approaching SuperCopter, sending it to a watery grave.

"Alex!"

Alex pulled his ComWatch up to his face. Valerie leaned in and looked at it with him. Commander Kellie's face was on the screen.

"Alex, can you guys do anything?!" she asked. "We're having to keep our distance! It's making it hard to get a clean shot!"

Alex looked at Valerie.

Valerie looked at Alex.

Sha-POWWWWWWWWWWW!!!!!

"We'll do what we can!" Valerie shouted into the ComWatch. She grabbed Alex's hand and asked, "Are you ready?"

Alex looked at Valerie warily. "Ready…for *what?*"

He got up on his knees, too.

"Well, I've been thinking. What this pirate ship is missing is some *cannonballs.*"

Valerie got to her feet and pulled Alex up with her.

"Valerie, have I mentioned that I don't ever want to be a human cann—"

"Aaaaaaaahhhhhhhhhhhhhhhh!!!!!!!" Valerie yelled, running forward. Alex, firmly grasping her hand, picked up his pace and gave in to her leading.

"Aaaaaaaahhhhhhhhhhhhhhhh!!!!!!!" he yelled with her.

With full force, the two Superkids barreled into Leblanc. "Cannonball!!!" they cried.

Sha-POWWWWWWWWWWW!!!!! The Paralyzer shot off again, this time missing its target.

As Valerie, Alex and Leblanc tumbled onto the deck in a tangled mass, Commander Kellie's voice shouted out of the ComWatch, "I don't know what you guys did, but good job! We're coming in!"

As the three struggled on the deck, Valerie heard the SuperCopters fly overhead, circling around.

"Get off of me!" Leblanc shouted. "Get *off!*"

With a burst of energy, the pirate shoved the Superkids away. He jumped up and back. Ophus ran forward to stop him, but halted in his tracks when Leblanc reached down and grabbed his silver knife off the deck.

"Ztand back!" he ordered. Everyone froze.

Leblanc's bird landed on his shoulder. "Donga donna shoot!" it squawked.

"Zhut up already about ze zhute!" Leblanc shouted at his parrot. It squawked again.

Leblanc backed up slowly as the SuperCopters circled overhead. He walked back to the ladder and crawled down the hole, threatening to knife anyone who dared to stop him.

"Where's he going?" Valerie wondered aloud.

Alex shook his head. "You don't think he's going to try and submerge, do you?"

Valerie looked at the open hatch into the ship. "Not likely," she said. "He'd sink himself."

"What then?" Alex asked.

BOOM! A SuperCopter landed on the deck and the side door popped open. Commander Kellie jumped out, her laser drawn. She pointed it at Ophus, but didn't fire.

"It's all right," Valerie said, running to her. "He's with us!"

Commander Kellie lowered her weapon and gave Valerie and Alex a quick hug. "Thank God, you're all right."

"God protected us," Valerie said.

"I had no doubt He would," the commander replied. "We've been praying for you since we lost contact with you yesterday."

Ophus stepped up and tapped Valerie on the shoulder. "Ophus knows where the Captain went," he said. Valerie turned and looked at him in wonderment.

"Where?" she asked.

Ophus stretched out his arm and pointed to the sea. "The Captain's going to use the *Sentry.*"

Valerie's brown eyes grew wide as she looked and saw Leblanc and his parrot plow out of the side of the coral ship, full speed ahead. The *Sentry* was small, but fast.

Commander Kellie clicked on her ComWatch. "Red 16, can you get a shot at that speedboat?"

"Working on it..." a male voice crackled back.

"He's getting away!" Alex shouted.

Valerie ran to the Paralyzer and grabbed the controls with both hands. "Not for long," she promised. Looking through the crosshairs, she aimed the device at the *Sentry.* When the crosshairs turned red and beeped, she knew her target was in her sights. She squeezed the trigger.

Sha-POWWWWWWWWWW!!!!! In brilliant green

light, the Paralyzer shot a beam that hit the *Sentry* dead center. At once, the small boat lost all power, skidding to a stop on the open ocean.

"Well done!" Commander Kellie congratulated. Alex clapped. Valerie's heart leapt. Leblanc was stopped! Valerie had stepped out in faith and—except for a few bruises and cuts—came out unscathed. God had protected her and she *hadn't* made a mistake. Valerie felt her eyes burning with tears. She had really done it!

"I'll bet you've got quite a story to tell," her commander said. Valerie hugged Commander Kellie again, holding back her tears. She shook hands with Alex. It was a job well done.

"Aaaggghhhh!"

Valerie, Commander Kellie, Alex and Ophus all looked out at Leblanc. He was in the *Sentry,* standing up, shouting. "Help! Help!" he cried.

Valerie's forehead wrinkled.

"What's he so upset about?" Alex wondered. "The sharks can't get him as long as he's in the boat..."

"It is coming apart!" the pirate hollered. "Ze *Zentry* is coming apart!"

Shark fins moved in his direction.

"Coming apart?" Valerie echoed. "I saw the *Sentry*

with my own eyes. It had nuts and bolts reinforcing the hull—that's impossible."

Ophus blushed.

Valerie's mouth dropped. "Ophus?"

He grinned.

"Ophus, do you know how that happened?"

The big lug broke into a wide smile. He took his fist out of the front pocket of his trousers and opened his meaty hand. Sitting inside was a pile of metal: nuts and bolts.

"Ophus!" Valerie scolded, breaking into a smile. "You shouldn't have—" she couldn't finish her sentence. She started laughing.

"It's all right," Commander Kellie comforted. "Our pilots will be able to get to him in time."

Valerie laughed and laughed. Commander Kellie and Alex joined in, too. Ophus barreled out his laughter above them all, his belly jiggling with every breath.

Overall, Valerie thought, it had been a pretty exciting 24 hours. As she watched the SuperCopters zip across the sky, she realized how much she really loved the adventure of being a Superkid. And one day, God willing, she would be a commander. God had protected her this far, and she knew He wouldn't let up. He would be with her throughout her calling, His footprints with hers every step of the way.

Valerie knew she had discovered something valuable that would stay with her for the remainder of her days. She had stepped out, at the risk of making a mistake—and won. God was able to handle any mistake she made and turn it into victory. God was able! And that's what really mattered. It wasn't Valerie's own ideas or *her* plans. It wasn't her mistakes…or even her future. All that mattered was *Jesus…Jesus.* He was the One Who made her complete. She would serve Him the rest of her days, with every bit of strength she had.

The past 24 hours had been filled with trials and tribulations, but Valerie had discovered that in her life, *God was able* to do far above what she could ask or think. It was a truth that she had discovered, not when she was fretting or fumbling or floundering—but when she was *faithful.* It was the truth she'd discovered when she was out of breath.

Epilogue

More than 1,000 miles from Superkid Academy, in the cheerful metropolis of Nautical, three Superkids looked forward to a restful Christmas vacation. Paul, Missy and Rapper exited the hovercab with wide smiles on their faces. They leisurely made their way up the wide, stone steps to the luxurious Ashton mansion—Missy's home.

Paul, an orphan, was thrilled to be invited to the Christmas festivities. Rapper, who was only staying for a few days before going to his own home, was looking forward to a little high-class R&R. Jet-powered spa, in-home theatre, self-cleaning bathroom—ah, the amenities. Missy was just happy to be home. After all that had happened over the past few months, she was excited beyond words to get back to "normalness," back to simplicity, back to the comforts of Mommy and Daddy. Home was the one safe haven where surely nothing odd would happen—where nothing out of the ordinary would throw her for a loop.

With each step up the walkway, lights turned on to signal their arrival. Two tall fountains, one on each side of the steps, spat crystal-clear water into the chilly air. Behind the trimmed bushes, behind the grand, white pillars on the porch and through a window, the velvet curtains pulled aside. Four eyes peered out above two happy smiles. Seconds later, the massive front door slid open and Gregg and Lois Ashton, Missy's parents, appeared.

Missy's mom, a slender, never-aging woman with long, blond curls and soft facial features, threw her hands out wide and exclaimed, "Tootle!"

Missy blushed as she set down her bags. She moved forward and hugged her mom happily.

"Tootle?" Rapper asked Paul.

Paul shook his head. "Don't ask," he said.

Rapper angled his thumb forward. "I didn't know Missy had a sister…" he wondered aloud.

"That's her *mom,* " Paul corrected. Rapper just nodded, not really very surprised.

Missy's dad hugged her next. He was about 6-feet tall with white, receding hair and a cleanshaven face. His bushy, white eyebrows raised as he chuckled and hugged his daughter.

Mrs. Ashton wasted no time making Paul and Rapper feel at home. She hugged Paul with a "So good to see you again!" and then introduced herself to Rapper. Mr. Ashton gave the same greeting, only with firm handshakes, and for Paul, a pat on the back. "It's good to be back," Paul replied truthfully each time.

"Come inside! Come inside! It's cold out here!" Mrs. Ashton beckoned, guiding each of the Superkids in front of herself.

As they entered, Missy's dad said, "Paul, we thought you could stay in the same room as last time and, Rapper, you can have your choice of the other five guest rooms."

Rapper looked at Paul, his eyebrows saying, *Five?!* louder than his words ever could. But with his mouth he said, "I can tell I'm going to like it here already."

Paul laughed. "You haven't seen anything yet," he said. The Superkids went inside. Lois Ashton followed, letting the electronic door slide shut automatically.

Across the lawn, hidden up in a thick oak tree that somehow, through the miracle of technology, still had all its leaves, two brown eyes stared out in an icy gaze. A wisp of black hair sailed across them, but they didn't blink. They just watched. Then, the right eyelid slightly closed as the lips curled into a sneer.

"Welcome home," the sinister voice mocked. "Welcome home."

To be continued...

'Twas the night before Christmas
and all through the house,
Not a creature was stirring…except
an NME ~~mouse~~. rat

*Look for Commander Kellie and the Superkids*SM
novel #8—

The Year Mashela Stole Christmas
by Christopher P.N. Maselli

Prayer for Salvation

Father God, I believe that Jesus is Your Son and that You raised Him from the dead for me. Jesus, I give my life to You. Right now, I make You the Lord of my life and choose to follow You forever. I love You and I know You love me. Thank You, Jesus, for giving me a new life. Thank You for coming into my heart and being my Savior. I am a child of God! Amen.

About the Author

Christopher P.N. Maselli is the author of the *Commander Kellie and the Superkids*$_{SM}$ Series. He also writes the bimonthly children's magazine, *Shout! The Voice of Victory for Kids,* and has contributed to the *Commander Kellie and the Superkids*$_{SM}$ movies.

Originally from Iowa and a graduate of Oral Roberts University, Chris now lives in Fort Worth, Texas, with his wife, Gena, where he is actively involved in the children's ministry at his local church. When he's not writing, he enjoys in-line skating, playing computer games and collecting Legos®.

Other Books Available

And Jesus Healed Them All (confession book and CD gift package)
Baby Praise Board Book
Baby Praise Christmas Board Book
Noah's Ark Coloring Book
The Best of *Shout!* Adventure Comics
The *Shout!* Giant Flip Coloring Book
The *Shout!* Joke Book
The *Shout!* Super-Activity Book
Wichita Slim's Campfire Stories

Commander Kellie and the Superkids $_{SM}$ **Books:**

The SWORD Adventure Book
Commander Kellie and the Superkids $_{SM}$ Solve-It-Yourself Mysteries
Commander Kellie and the Superkids $_{SM}$ Adventure Series: Middle Grade Novels by Christopher P.N. Maselli:

#1 The Mysterious Presence
#2 The Quest for the Second Half
#3 Escape From Jungle Island
#4 In Pursuit of the Enemy
#5 Caged Rivalry
#6 Mystery of the Missing Junk
#7 Out of Breath
#8 The Year Mashela Stole Christmas

World Offices of Kenneth Copeland Ministries

For more information about KCM and a free catalog, please write the office nearest you:

Kenneth Copeland Ministries
Fort Worth, Texas 76192-0001

Kenneth Copeland
Locked Bag 2600
Mansfield Delivery Centre
QUEENSLAND 4122
AUSTRALIA

Kenneth Copeland
Post Office Box 15
BATH
BA1 3XN
ENGLAND U.K.

Kenneth Copeland
Private Bag X 909
FONTAINEBLEAU
2032
REPUBLIC OF SOUTH AFRICA

Kenneth Copeland
Post Office Box 378
Surrey, B.C.
V3T 5B6
CANADA

Kenneth Copeland Ministries
Post Office Box 84
L'VIV 79000
UKRAINE